拆解
易混淆英語

蔡英材 編著

DON'T GET MIXED UP

商務印書館

責任編輯	黃家麗
裝幀設計	趙穎珊
排　版	高向明
責任校對	趙會明
印　務	龍寶祺

拆解易混淆英語 *Don't get mixed up*

作　者：蔡英材

出　版：商務印書館 (香港) 有限公司
　　　　香港筲箕灣耀興道 3 號東滙廣場 8 樓
　　　　http://www.commercialpress.com.hk

發　行：香港聯合書刊物流有限公司
　　　　香港新界荃灣德士古道 220-248 號荃灣工業中心 16 樓

印　刷：寶華數碼印刷有限公司
　　　　香港柴灣吉勝街勝景工業大廈 4 樓 A 室

版　次：2024 年 7 月第 1 版第 1 次印刷
　　　　© 2024 商務印書館 (香港) 有限公司
　　　　ISBN 978 962 07 4699 4
　　　　Printed in Hong Kong

Contents 目錄

前言 *Introduction*

　　首先，非常感謝大家閱讀本書，我衷心希望本書有助你提升英語水平。書內收錄的典型錯誤來自日常生活的商業信函、會議紀錄、廣告、啟事、通告、宣傳品和其他文件的實際例子，通過詳細解釋，讓大家明白出錯的原因，避免犯錯，增加學習及工作的信心。

　　為甚麼要學好英文？英語作為世界通行的語言，功用也不用詳細說明。香港某教育集團每年都公佈全球 88 個非英語國家及地區的英語能力指標結果，多年前香港排名三十，雖然屬中級水平，卻被位列第三的新加坡大幅拋離，比菲律賓、馬來西亞及印度等亞洲國家的排名更低。對於該報告是否具有權威性，我不作評論，但英語水平一直下降則絕對是事實。

　　由於我是退休講師，也許可在這裏分享一點教育方面的體驗。現時大多數家長為了培養子女成為精英，從小會為他們鋪路，由幼兒班、幼稚園、小學以至中學，家長都會想盡辦法幫助子女入讀名校，特別是以英語為授課語言的名校，希望兒女年年名列前茅，在中學文憑試科科考獲 5**，然後進入心儀的大學，畢業後找到高薪厚職。但沒法進入名校的學生，有些很早就放棄學業，可能其他各科僅僅及格，惟獨英語科成績不及格。更令人婉惜的是，九年免費教育制度令這些程度不高的學生每年升級，結果考中學文憑試科科不及格。

　　另一方面，現時學生在公開試英文科無法取得優良成績，大多數是因為錯誤太多被扣分。因此，只要大家正確運用英語，注意避免詞彙和句子方面的錯誤，成績就會變好。本書針對日

常例子並且提供練習題，希望能夠幫助大家愉快學習。

　　雖然香港的雙語政策不像新加坡那樣明顯，但政府部門、私人機構和跨國公司在公事上大多使用英文，連著名大學都是以英文為授課語言，這是鐵一般的事實。當然，沒有良好英語基礎的學生將來的前途不一定黯淡，但在升學和就業方面無可避免受到一些限制。另一個可怕的事實是，隨着二十年多來香港的大學學位大幅增加，普通畢業生的就業情況越來越不理想。今時今日，像普通一份適合大學生申請的政府或大機構的職位往往吸引成千上萬的申請人，在「過五關，斬六將」的過程中，英語能力測試的殺傷力最大，很多申請人因為英語部分錯誤太多而被淘汰，但更殘酷的是，政府或大機構近年聘請員工時，要求申請人需有較高的中英文程度，例如要求中學文憑試 3, 4, 5 或 5* 級 / CRE 中文或英文運用試卷一級或二級。然而，英語程度不高的學生不用因為成績不好而感到頹喪，只管努力學好英語就可以。要學好英語，永不言棄才是正確的態度。

蔡英材

中文思維
引起混淆

1.1 一個字母 s 也可決定對錯

在中文商業文件裏，經常出現「如下」這個中文詞語，而對應的英文是 <u>as follows</u>，但很多時候大家會誤寫成 *as follow。

其實 <u>as follows</u> 才是正確的，因為它的全寫是 <u>as (it) follows</u>，省略了中間的 <u>it</u>，所以很容易誤寫成 *as follow。例如：

結果如下：X, Y 和 Z。

  ✔ The results are <u>as follows</u>: X, Y and Z.

開放時間如下：

  ✔ The opening hours are <u>as follows</u>:

最重要的是：<u>as follows</u> 即使後面跟着幾個名詞也必須保持不變，不應把 <u>as follows</u> 誤寫成 *as follow。

得獎者如下：陳大衛、黃彼德及張瑪莉。

  ✔ The winners are <u>as follows</u>: David Chan, Peter Wong and Mary Cheung.

同樣，無論 <u>as follows</u> 前面是單數還是複數，它都不會改變。例如：

  ✔ The rule is <u>as follows</u>:

  ✔ The rules are as follows:

把它寫成 *The rule is as follow: 或 *The rules are as follow: 都

不對。

其他正確例子還有：

詳情如下：

✓ The details are <u>as follows</u>:

她收到一張字條，內容如下：

✓ She received a note which read <u>as follows</u>:

委員會仍有五個空缺尚未填補：

✓ There remain five unfilled vacancies on the Commission <u>as follows</u>:

委員會成員如下：

✓ Membership of the Commission is <u>as follows</u>:

她收到一張字條，內容如下：

✓ She received a note which read <u>as follows</u>:

委員會仍有五個空缺尚未填補：

✓ There remain five unfilled vacancies on the Commission <u>as follows</u>:

委員會成員如下：

✓ Membership of the Commission is <u>as follows</u>:

1.2 「以下指引」是 below guidelines 嗎？

許多文件經常出現 <u>below</u>，是「以下」的意思，例如「以下指引、規則、說明、資料」，但是 *<u>below</u> guidelines / rules / instructions / information 都是錯誤的。

因為 <u>below</u> 是副詞，不是形容詞，把它放在名詞前面是錯誤的。正確用法是：

以下指引	✔ Guidelines <u>below</u>
以下規則	✔ Rules <u>below</u>
以下說明	✔ Instructions <u>below</u>
以下資料	✔ Information <u>below</u>

大家把 <u>below</u> 放在名詞前面，可能以為它是介詞，但這也是錯的，因為「以下」不等於「在……的下面、低於」的意思。例如：

女孩子在冬天應穿長及膝蓋下的裙子。

> ✔ Girls should wear skirts that reach <u>below</u> the knees in winter.

他們潛入水中。

> ✔ They dived <u>below</u> the surface of the water.

十一歲以下的兒童不准入內。

✔ No entry to children <u>below</u> the age of eleven.

她的表現大大低於一般水平。

✔ Her performance is well <u>below</u> average.

其實，大家若想把「以下」的英文放在名詞前面的話，可以改用形容詞 <u>following</u>。

例如：

付款可用以下方法。

✔ Payment may be made in the <u>following</u> ways.

1.3 看管隨身物品用 beware of 正確嗎？

我們經常看見有些告示牌寫着 <u>beware</u> ... 來提醒別人提防某些危險可能出現，例如「內有惡犬」的警告，英文是 <u>beware of</u> the dog，但注意不是 ✗ <u>beware</u> the dog。其他例子還有：

當心曬日光浴時睡着。

✗ <u>Beware</u> falling asleep when sunbathing.

✓ <u>Beware of</u> falling asleep when sunbathing.

小心路滑。

✗ <u>Beware</u> slippery roads.

✓ <u>Beware of</u> slippery roads.

又例如：

小心求職陷阱。

✓ <u>Beware of</u> employment traps.

提防小手。

✓ <u>Beware of</u> pickpockets.

提防石頭掉下。

✓ <u>Beware of</u> falling rocks.

她告訴他提防自己的太太嗎？

✓ Was she telling him to <u>beware of</u> his wife?

小心別草率決定。

  ✔ <u>Beware of</u> making hasty decisions.

! NOTES 注意 !

我們把 <u>beware</u> 用作看管(take care of)的意思時，它是及物動詞，後面連接賓語。

小心你的錢包。

  ✘ <u>Beware of</u> your wallet.

  ✔ <u>Beware</u> your wallet.

1.4 「身體檢查」原來不該説 body-check

大家聽到 body-check 的時候，一定會覺得它沒有錯，因為我們日常生活説的「身體檢查」，英文不就是 body-check 嗎？雖然很多人會説 body-check，但它並不正確。為甚麼呢？

其實，body 有多個意思，除了解作「身體、軀體、主體、團體、物體」之外，還有「屍體」，而西方人的日常生活裏，一説到 body 多是「屍體、死屍」的意思，即 dead body。在以前流行的美國電視片集 CSI 裏，鑑證人員經常説的 We found a body. 就是「發現死屍」的意思。

以下是 body 解作「身體」的常用例子：

體脂 / 體重 / 體溫 body fat / weight / temperature

健身 body building

體臭 body odour

搜身 body search

身體語言 body language

體重指數 body mass index (BMI)

其他用語還有：

保鑣 body guard

生物鐘 body clock

運屍袋 body bag

body-check 的另一個解釋是「身體阻截、身體阻擋」的意思，屬冰球用語。

至於「身體／健康檢查」，我們可以說 check-up、physical check-up。「全身檢查」是 general check-up、「產前檢查」是 antenatal check-up、「牙醫檢查」是 dental check-up。

1.5 改衣是 change clothes 嗎？

近十多年來，隨着電腦科技日益發展，線上翻譯非常流行，以致很多人翻譯時經常倚賴各類翻譯軟件。但大家很快體會到使用這些軟件翻譯的缺點，原來它只是做配對（matching）工作。英譯中的時候，還可以勉強理解，像「我困在升降機內」，即使誤譯成 *I was sleepy in the lift. ，我們也知道譯錯了，因為只要用英文做 back translation 就不難明白確實有錯。至於中文翻譯，有些錯誤會令人捧腹大笑，例如 I have butterflies in my stomach. 會誤譯成「＊我肚裏有蝴蝶。」、make yourself at home 誤譯成「＊令你自己在家」、be my guest 誤譯成「＊成為我的客人」、help yourself 竟然是「＊救救自己」、I am good 是「＊我好」、see you 成為「＊看你」、俚語 bite me 竟然是「＊咬我」、shoot 就成為「射」等等。

總之，胡亂直譯或死譯是學好英文的重大障礙，此外，我們必須努力避免「中式英語」。就像中文的「改」，它主要是「更改、改變、變化」的意思。一般來説，它的英文是 change。例如：

春天有些樹葉由綠變紅。

In spring, some leaves change from green to red.

交通燈改變（為紅色）時要停下來。

Stop when the traffic lights change (to red).

自從我上次和他見面以來，他變了很多。

He has changed a lot since I last saw him.

她改了我們的上課時間。

She has changed the time of our lesson.

但中文裏「改」還有別的意思。

例如「改衣服」就是「改動、修改」衣服的意思。很多服裝店經常説提供改衣服務，但英文不是 change clothes 而是 alter clothes。例如：

這裙子需要改一改。它太緊了。

The dress will have to be altered. It is too tight.

它的名詞是 alteration。例如：

我的襯衣需要改一下。

My shirt needs alteration.

我們必須明白 change clothes 是「換、更換衣服」的意思，不是「改衣」。例如：

他的新外衣不合身，因此他拿回店裏換了（一件）。

His new coat doesn't fit so he took it back to the shop and changed it (for another).

她在商店換了幾本書。

She changed some books at the shop.

1.6 Chair vs Stool ——不是所有櫈都叫 Chair

記得兒時大牌檔很普遍，幾乎遍佈舊區的街頭巷尾。初時只有木枱和木櫈，後來改為摺枱和摺櫈，最普遍是圓形的。這些摺枱、摺櫈非常實用，加上收藏容易，所以十分受歡迎，當年差不多每個家庭都會購置。

但大家要注意這些櫈不是 chair，而大牌檔的摺櫈不是 folding chair。以下是一些錯誤例子：

那些熟食檔摺櫈不安全。

> ✘ The folding chairs at cooked food stores are not safe.

那些熟食檔摺櫈可以用作武器。

> ✘ The folding chairs at cooked food stores can be used as weapons.

其實，即使是現在的木櫈和其他櫈如廚房櫈、鋼琴櫈及酒吧櫈，只要它們是沒有背的，它們都不是 chair。

! NOTES 注意 !

英文的 chair 是有背的椅子，沒有背的就不是 chair。沒有背的櫈英文是 stool，因為 A stool is a seat without a back.。

所以上述兩句應改為：

那些熟食檔摺櫈不安全。

　　✓ The folding stools at cooked food stores are not safe.

那些熟食檔摺櫈可以用作武器。

　　✓ The folding stools at cooked food stores can be used as weapons.

其他例子還有：

　　木櫈 a wooden stool

　　鋼琴櫈 a piano stool

　　酒吧櫈 a bar stool

! NOTES 注意 !

我們在酒樓和餐廳給嬰兒坐的不是 stool，這些有背的嬰兒櫈是 <u>high chair</u>。

1.7 「商店休息」不是 Close 和 We're close，為甚麼？

我們逛街時，經常看到商店大門掛上「休息」的標誌，但英文經常出現 Close 和 We're close。那是不對的。為甚麼呢？

這是因為 close 是動詞，形容詞是 closed。

closed 是「關上」的意思。例如：

張開嘴巴，閉上眼睛。

✔ Open your mouth and <u>close</u> your eyes.

商店八點鐘關門。

✔ The shop <u>closes</u> at eight o'clock.

銀行明天下午二時停止營業。

✔ The bank <u>closes</u> at 2 p.m. tomorrow.

大多數圖書館星期一關門。

✔ Many libraries <u>close</u> on Mondays.

那馬路 / 邊境 / 機場 / 公園關閉了。

✔ The road / border / airport / park is <u>closed</u>.

超級市場今天不開門。

✔ The supermarket is <u>closed</u> today.

會議在閉門情況下進行。

✔ The meeting was held behind <u>closed</u> doors.

閉路電視

✔ <u>closed</u> circuit television (CCTV)

但不要忘記：<u>close</u> 也是形容詞和副詞，但它的意思不同，它是「靠近、離開不遠」的意思。例如：

銀行離商店不遠。

✔ The bank is <u>close</u> to the shops.

測驗日期近在眼前。

✔ The test is getting very <u>close</u>.

不要太靠近。

✔ Don't come too <u>close</u>.

他們緊挨着坐在一起。

✔ They sat <u>close</u> together.

1.8 還未回到公司，說 has not come back 正確嗎？

如果接到電話找某同事，但他還沒有回到辦公室，我們就很容易會說 He hasn't <u>come</u> back yet. 。不過這是錯的，因為 <u>come</u> back / return to work 是指經過一段較長時間缺席，如在午膳或假期之後上班等。

我們如要說某人早上仍未回到辦公室，應說 He hasn't <u>come</u> in yet. 或 He hasn't <u>come</u> to work yet. 。「早上回到工作崗位」是 go / <u>come</u> to work in the morning。

在其他辦公時間說某人不在工作崗位時，應說 He is not <u>in</u>.。

! NOTES 注意 *!*

我們說某人未回到工作崗位，不是說 *He hasn't returned to work.，因為這錯誤等於 He hasn't <u>come</u> back to work.。

其他正確例子還有：

他病假後今天上班。

> He <u>returned to work</u> today after his sick leave.

暑假完了 —— 我們要返回校園了。

> Summer vacation is over – we have to <u>go back to</u> school.

我們剛從泰國回來。

We have just <u>come back from</u> Thailand.

總之，我們不說：

早上我們回辦公室上班。

✘ We return to work in the morning.

午飯後她回辦公室上班。

✘ She comes to work after lunch.

1.9 I enjoy your company. 千萬別以為是「我喜歡你公司。」

學習英語其中的一個困難，是遇到「一詞多義」的情況，以 <u>company</u> 為例，相信很多人都知道它解作「公司」，這個意思用得非常廣泛，但其實 company 還有「在一起、陪伴」的意思，特別是在英語會話裏，它是十分常用的。例如：

我喜歡和蘇珊在一起。

✔ I enjoy Susan's <u>company</u>.

他喜愛獨自遠足。

✔ He enjoys his own <u>company</u> when he is hiking.

她不知道他有客人。

✔ She didn't realise he had <u>company</u>.

謝謝你與我一起。

✔ Thank you for your <u>company</u>.

安琪兒很高興有這隻狗作伴。

✔ Angela was glad to have the dog as <u>company</u>.

我感謝有她作伴。

✔ I was grateful for her <u>company</u>.

他不反對我陪伴他。

✔ He had no objection to my <u>company</u>.

你想人陪？

✔ You want some <u>company</u>?

我們看到以上例子，請別誤會它解作「公司」。事實上，上述句子都是實用的日常英語，我們只要多加練習，英語水平就會提高。其他正確例子如下：

好夥伴、人緣好的人

✔ Good <u>company</u>

壞朋友

✔ Bad <u>company</u>

當着別人面前

✔ In <u>company</u>

1.10 「異性約會對象」英文怎樣説？

有一次我在外語電視劇聽到 Where is my <u>date</u>?，中文字幕竟是「我的日期在哪裏？」。它當然是錯的。

在日常英語會話裏，我們經常説 date，它是名詞。很多人都知道它是「日期」的意思，可惜大家可能不知道它非正式的意思是「異性間的社交約會」及「約會的對象」，後者即廣東話「拖友」的意思，它是常用美語。其他例子還有：

你父母讓你出去與異性約會嗎？

Do your parents let you go out on <u>dates</u>?

明天晚上我與瑪莉有個約會。

I've got a <u>date</u> with Mary tomorrow night.

朝思暮想的約會

Hot <u>date</u>

相親（即由第三者安排的男女初次約會）

Blind <u>date</u>

你會把你約會的對象帶來參加聚會嗎？

Will you bring your <u>date</u> to the party?

我約了對象晚上六時見面。

My <u>date</u> is meeting me at 6 p.m.

我的男 / 女朋友在哪裏？

Where is my date?

date 也是動詞，它是美語，是「與人約會」的意思，即廣東話的「拍拖」。例如：

他與瑪麗約會已有數年。

He's been dating Mary for several years.

! NOTES 注意 !

date 是社交約會或與異性互相約會，不是公事上的約會或預約，那是 appointment。

我想預約一下，星期五來找黃醫生看病。

I would like to make an appointment to see Dr. Wong this Friday.

他往赴一個約會，跟校長共晉午餐。

He went out for a lunch appointment with the principal.

1.11 「麻木」、「僵局」都可用 dead

在日常生活裏，英語 dead 很常用，它是形容詞，是人、動物或植物「死」的意思。例如：

我以為他已經死了。

I thought he was <u>dead</u>.

他在槍戰中被擊斃。

He was shot <u>dead</u> in a gunfight.

露絲把枯死的花扔了。

Lucy threw away the <u>dead</u> flowers.

他們發現三具屍體。

They found three <u>dead</u> bodies.

以下是特別的用法：

我的手指麻木了。

My fingers have gone <u>dead</u>.

不知道今晚哪兒不對勁，我實在累死了。

I don't know what's wrong tonight, I'm absolutely <u>dead</u>.

冬季大部份度假勝地都很冷清。

Most holiday resorts are <u>dead</u> during the winter.

我們正在通話時手提電話中斷了。

The mobile phone went <u>dead</u> in the middle of our conversations.

僵局

<u>dead</u> end

冗員、廢物

<u>dead</u> wood

突然死了（暴斃）

dropped <u>dead</u>

廢電池

<u>dead</u> battery

另一方面，當我們說一個人死了，除非是在過去的情況說，否則在目前情況說一個人死了，我們應該用現在式，不可說 He was <u>dead</u>.，否則別人會以為他重生了，還生存到現在。即死過翻生。正確例子是：

祖父死了，他是 2001 年去世的。

✓ My grandfather is <u>dead</u>; he died in 2001.

dead

1.12 except 和 beside 要分清楚

我們經常說「除了……以外」(except)，但使用 except 很容易出錯。以下是錯誤例子：

除了彼德以外，沒有人反對建議 (只有彼德反對)。

> ✘ Besides Peter, no one objects.

我們應該説：

> ✔ No one objects to the proposal except (for) Peter. 或
> ✔ Except for Peter, no one objects to the proposal.

為甚麼呢？那是因為 except 是指不屬句子所指的物件、事情或人。它不像中文的用法，是不常用於句子開頭的。如要放在句子開頭，我們要用 except for。其他例子還有：

除了星期三傍晚以外，勞倫斯通常有空。

Except for Wednesday evenings, Lawrence is free anytime.

除了水以外，任何東西都可以塞住去水口。

Anything, except water, is likely to block an outlet.

除了蘇珊以外，所有女孩子都笑了起來。

All the girls except Susan started to laugh.

除了他以外，我沒有真正喜歡的人。

There's nobody that I really like, except him.

除了她以外，大衛沒有准許任何人進入房間。

David had allowed no one to enter the room <u>except</u> her.

此外，在 all、any、every、no、everything、anybody、nowhere、nobody、whole 這類概括性詞語後面，經常省略 for。例如：

除了榴槤以外，他吃掉桌上所有東西。

He ate everything on the table <u>except</u> the durian.

除了約翰和瑪麗以外，誰也沒有來。

Nobody came <u>except</u> (for) John and Mary.

至於 ✘ Besides Peter, no one objects to the proposal，這句不正確，這是因為 besides 是「除了……還／還有」in addition to 的意思。例如：

除了中英文，你還懂甚麼語言？

What languages do you know <u>besides</u> Chinese and English?

除了「武士之星」，他還有三匹馬。

He has three horses <u>besides</u> Knight.

1.13 水電費、巴士費、律師費等不可用 expenses

在日常生活裏，我們經常要負擔各種費用及開支，例如水費、電費、煤氣費、電話費、交通費、生活費、律師費、醫療開支、家庭開支等，因而使用 expenses、fee、fare 及 bill 時出現混亂，錯誤例子如下：

水費

✗ Water <u>expenses / fee</u>

電費

✗ Electricity <u>expenses / fee</u>

煤氣費

✗ Gas <u>expenses / fee</u>

電話費

✗ Telephone <u>expenses / fee</u>

造成上述錯誤的原因，主要是因為我們經常把「水費單」、「電費單」、「煤氣費單」及「電話費單」說成「交水費」、「交電費」、「交煤氣費」、「交電話費」，因而忘記 pay the water <u>bill</u>、pay the electricity <u>bill</u>、pay the gas <u>bill</u> 及 pay the phone <u>bill</u> 才是正確的說法。

另一原因是我們誤以為中文的「費」是 <u>expenses</u> 或 <u>fee</u>。但其

實 expenses 及 fee 是有指定意義或固定用法的。例如：

交通費

travelling expenses

生活費

living expenses

殮葬費

funeral expenses

家庭 / 醫療開支

household / medical expenses

fee 是專業人士如會計師、醫生、律師及政府牌照的費用和會費、學費、入場費、登記費、顧問費、董事袍金等。例如：doctors' fees 是醫生費，legal fees 是訴訟費。

! NOTES 注意 !

公共交通工具例如飛機、的士、巴士、電車的費用是 fare，而隧道費是 toll。

1.14 廣東話「地下」是 floor 還是 ground ？

某電視台中文頻道的一個旅遊節目介紹亞洲某國家的咖啡種植園。當園主帶着節目主持人四處參觀時，其中一個主持人突然向着馬路旁邊一大堆咖啡豆說 You can see coffee beans on the <u>floor</u> of the road. ，嚇了我一跳。

沒錯 <u>floor</u> 是「地面」的意思，因此我們可以說：

她每天打掃廚房的地。

She sweeps the kitchen <u>floor</u> every day.

落地燈

floor lamp

樓層平面圖

floor plan

但我們必須明白：<u>floor</u> 是指鋪上物料的地面，即木質、水泥、磚塊、大理石等地面，即 wooden / concrete / marble <u>floor</u>。馬路沒有鋪上任何物料的地面是 <u>ground</u>。英文解釋是 the solid surface of the earth that you walk on。由於 <u>floor</u> 和 <u>ground</u> 的廣東話都是「地」，所以一說到「地」，就會混淆 <u>floor</u> 和 <u>ground</u>。錯誤例子如下：

我們坐在客廳地板上看電視。

✘ We were sitting on the <u>ground</u> in the living room watching TV.

既然我們説客廳，客廳哪裏有 <u>ground</u> 呢？所以應該是 <u>floor</u>。

她把手袋掉在公路的地上。

✘ She dropped the handbag on the <u>floor</u> in the highway.

這也是錯的，因為手袋掉在公路上的地面，所以應該説 <u>ground</u>。

他躺在地上。

He was lying on the <u>floor</u> / <u>ground</u>.

這句用 <u>floor</u> 或 <u>ground</u> 都可以。如果是室內，應説 <u>floor</u>。馬路的路面應是 <u>ground</u>。

> # ! *NOTES* 注意 !
>
> 室內的地面用 <u>floor</u>，室外的地面用 <u>ground</u>.

其他例子還有：

直升機離地幾分鐘便墜毀了。

The helicopter crashed a few minutes after it left the <u>ground</u>.

擦地布

<u>floor</u> cloth

場記

<u>floor</u> manager

1.15 「今後」、「將來」用 in future 還是 in the future？

在日常生活裏，我們經常説「將來」，英語是 <u>future</u>，但經常會不小心混淆了 <u>in the future</u> 和 <u>in future</u>。以下是錯誤例子：

要保證以後準時到達那裏。

✘ <u>In future</u>, make sure you will get there on time.

今後它不會發生。

✘ It will not take place <u>in the future</u>.

他們擔心以後不知道會進展至甚麼情況。

✘ They worried what would happen <u>in future</u>.

以後你應早點完成。

✘ <u>In future</u>, try to finish earlier.

將來她想成為護士。

✘ She hopes to be a nurse <u>in future</u>.

出現上述錯誤主要是大家不能區分 <u>in future</u> 和 <u>in the future</u>。

請記着 <u>in future</u> 是「今後、以後」，等於 from now on；<u>in the future</u> 才是「將來」的意思。例如：

今後門要鎖好。

In future, make sure the door is locked.

將來她希望取得律師資格。

In the future, she hopes to qualify as a lawyer.

以後所有報告都必須寄到澳洲。

In future, all reports must be sent to Australia.

希望將來會採取更多安全措施。

It was hoped that more safety measures would be taken in the future.

今後請加倍小心。

Please be more careful in future.

! NOTES 注意 !

注意：在美式英語，in the future 也是 in future 的意思。In the distant future 是「在久遠的未來」，in the near future 是「近期」的意思。

1.16 單數和複數動詞的使用規則

不少人不明白單數和複數名詞怎樣影響動詞的使用，所以我在這裏談談單數和複數動詞的使用規則。

其實，單數和複數動詞的使用規則很易明白，只要動詞前面的名詞是單數，就應該用單數動詞。同樣，如果動詞前面的名詞是複數，就應該用複數動詞。

但大家仍經常弄不明白，請看以下的錯誤例子：

私家車數目正在增加。

✗ The number of cars are increasing.

花園裏只有一些人。

✗ There is only a few people in the garden.

有些警員穿着制服，其餘的穿便服。

✗ Some of the policemen are in uniform, the rest is wearing plain clothes.

今天所有消息都很好。

✗ All the news are good today.

解釋如下：

例子 1

    ✘ Hong Kong have many tall buildings.

    ✔ Hong Kong has many tall buildings.

這類錯誤很簡單。既然 Hong Kong 是單數，便不應該用 have，應該改用 has。「動詞」have 應該在「主語」是複數時才用（除非「主語」是 I）。

例子 2

    ✘ The number of private cars are increasing.

    ✔ The number of private cars is increasing.

這句的問題在於大家弄不清楚主語是甚麼。如果大家以為 private cars 是主語，便會錯用 are 來描述它。其實，這句的主語是 number。我們說的是「私家車數目正在增加」，強調「數目正在增加」，不是「私家車正在增加」。正因為英文中 number 是單數，所以應該用 is 來描述它。

例子 3

    ✘ There is only a few people in the garden.

    ✔ There are only a few people in the garden.

這句跟例子 2 差不多，也是主語的單複數問題。當然這句的主語是 people，但大家可能忽略 people 雖然沒有加上 s，但本身具有複數的意義。

例子 4

  ✘ Some of the policemen are in uniform, the rest is wearing plain clothes.

  ✔ Some of the policemen are in uniform, the rest are wearing plain clothes.

例子 4 的問題主要出在 the rest 上，因為 rest 看起來是單數，所以我們便會用 is。犯這樣的錯誤純粹由於不明白這裏的 the rest 是指 the rest of the policemen。既然 policemen 是複數，那麼「其餘的」(policemen) 也應該具有複數意義。

例子 5

  ✘ All the news are good today.

  ✔ All the news is good today.

例子 5 出錯的原因很簡單。大家看到了 news，便以為它是複數。實際上英文有很多「名詞」是「天生」以 s 結尾的，s 是它必不可少的組成部份，查閱字典就可以確認這類「名詞」的單複數。

其實，單數和複數名詞與單數和複數名詞的配合，就是英語語法所指的 agreement 即「一致性」。

1. 所謂 agreement「一致性」，是指英文句子中的「動詞」必須與其「主語」一致，即單數「名詞」配單數形式的「動詞」，複數「名詞」配複數形式的「動詞」。以下是一些簡單例子：

is / are	My manager <u>is</u> old.
	My managers <u>are</u> old.
has / have	David <u>has</u> an office.
	My friend and I <u>have</u> an office.
do / does	<u>Does</u> he work in Central?
	<u>Do</u> they work in Central?
this / these	<u>This</u> pen is mine.
	<u>These</u> pens are mine.
that / those	<u>That</u> lift is big.
	<u>Those</u> lifts are big.
simple present tense	He <u>lives</u> here.
	They <u>live</u> here.

2. 留意在 There / where is / are... 的句式中,「動詞」必須與它後面的「主語」一致。

房間有個男人。

<u>There</u> is a man in the room.

辦公室裏有幾位女士。

<u>There</u> are several ladies in the office.

其他錢在哪兒?

<u>Where</u> is the rest of the money?

其他工人在哪兒？

<u>Where</u> are the rest of the workers?

3. A lot of +不可數「名詞」+單數用的「動詞」；A lot of +複數可數「名詞」+複數用的「動詞」。

這塊肉很多地方腐爛了。

<u>A lot of</u> this meat is bad.

很多橘子壞了。

<u>A lot of</u> the oranges are bad.

瓶子裏有很多水。

There is <u>a lot of</u> water in the bottle.

街上有很多警車。

There are <u>a lot of</u> police cars in the street.

在語法使用上，every 和 each 限定、修飾的「名詞」要用單數形式，配以單數用的「動詞」。

這個中心裏每個學生都不到 12 歲。

<u>Every</u> student in this centre is under the age of twelve.

所有準備都做好了。

<u>Everything</u> is ready.

遇到 a pair of 要很小心，例如：

這副眼鏡很貴。

This <u>pair</u> of glasses is expensive.

這些眼鏡很貴。

These glasses are expensive.

那把剪刀很鋒利。

That <u>pair</u> of scissors is sharp.

那些剪刀很鋒利。

Those scissors are sharp.

6. 句中出現 ... percent、majority 和 half of 時,「動詞」應視乎所指的「名詞」是單數還是複數而定。例如:

   a) The majority of this meat (肉:單數) is bad.

   b) The majority of these oranges (橙 / 橘子:複數) are bad.

   c) Half of this meat (肉:單數) is rotten.

   d) Half of these apples (蘋果:複數) are rotten.

   e) Fifty percent of this article (文章:單數) is irrelevant.

   f) Fifty percent of your answers (答案:複數) are correct.

理論上來說,"none" = 0。它不是單數,也不是複數。

但現在的語法專家認為使用複數較為普遍,「動詞」則應視乎「名詞」是單數還是複數而定。例如:

a) None of the students (學生：複數) are pleased with their result.

b) None of this money (錢：單數 / 不可數名詞) is ours.

people 表面上是單數，但實際上是複數。例如：

有些人正在等着見主席。

Some people are waiting to see the Chairman.

「人」的單數是 person ，例如：

每個人能分到的錢不多。

There is not much money for one person.

在正式的文體中， person 可以加 s 成為 persons ，例如：

炸彈爆炸令 123 人喪生。

The bomb exploded killing 123 persons.

! NOTES 注意 !

請記着，我們見到單數的「名詞」和「不可數名詞」應該用單數形式的「動詞」。

同樣，見到複數的「名詞」便應該用複數形式的「動詞」；一般來説，「可數名詞」結尾有 s 就代表複數，特殊的詞語除外。

1.17 時間詞是分辨 present perfect tense 和 past tense 的關鍵

在公營機構及私人公司經常收到市民或客人的來信，回信的時候，第一句通常是「謝謝你 X 月 X 日的來信。」Thank you for your letter of XXX. 或「你 X 月 XX 日的大函收悉。」，但注意後者的英文不是 *We have received your letter of 15 July。這是因為我們很多時混淆現在完成式和過去式，因而犯錯。

現在完成式和過去式的區別，就是使用現在完成式的句子裏，沒有時間詞顯示或證明動作或事情，即是如果句裏有時間詞顯示或證明相關動作或事情在過去發生，就應該用過去式，否則就應該用現在完成式來表示已完成的動作或事情。以下是使用過去式的例子：

她上星期寫信給他們。

She <u>wrote</u> to them <u>last week</u>.

那意外兩個星期前發生。

The accident <u>happened</u> <u>two weeks ago</u>.

今早你回來上班時見到彼德嗎？

<u>Did</u> you see Peter this morning when you <u>came to work</u>?

我去了該銀行但它關了門。

I <u>went</u> to the bank but it <u>was closed</u>.

在上述例子，因為各句都有時間詞顯示或證明相關動作或事情

確實在過去發生，所以使用過去式。

現在看看使用現在完成式的例子：

你填好申請表嗎？

Have you completed the application form yet?

她已／剛把計劃告訴彼德。

She has already / just spoken to Peter about the plan.

他向經理報告了嗎？

Has he made a report to the manager?

我們留意到……

It has come to our attention that...

從 2021 年他便在這部門工作。

He has worked in the department since 2021.

他在這部門工作了 10 年。

He has worked in the department for 10 years.

以上例子因沒有時間詞顯示或證明動作或事情確實在過去已完成，所以不應該用 past tense，特別是如果句裏有 yet、already、just、since（固定時間）和 for（一段時間），就應該用現在完成式。

1.18 注意有些名詞如 change、work 用作複數時意思會改變

寫英文文章時，要決定某個名詞是單數還是複數不太容易，可能產生很多不必要的錯誤，例如：

我們的總部在東京。

✘ Our headquarter is in Tokyo.

運動商品

✘ Sports good

今天有新消息嗎？

✘ Any new today?

剪刀在哪裏？

✘ Where is the scissor?

我不喜歡辦公室政治。

✘ I don't like office politic.

上述例子裏，名詞都應該改為 headquarters、goods、news、scissors 和 politics。

! *NOTES* 注意 !

英語裏必須有 s 的常用名詞還有 congratulations、barracks、news、economics、mathematics、physics、trousers、pants、scissors、jeans、pajamas、socks 和 shorts 等。

其實，對於這些名詞，我們無需問它們為甚麼不是單數，我們只要牢記它們就可以。

另一方面，英文有些名詞只有單數，沒有複數。同樣，我們無需問它們為甚麼沒有複數，我們只要牢記它們就可以。下列名詞只有單數：

furniture	information	advice	luggage	equipment
traffic	homework	housework	water	bread
dust	smoke	rice	cheese	butter
petrol	alcohol	evidence	knowledge	the following
trouble				

總之在這些名詞後面加上 s 成為複數是錯誤的。

當然，最麻煩的是一些只有單數的名詞，它們解作單數時沒有複數形式，但問題是它們可以變成複數，變成複數時意思又不同，所以要特別小心使用。例如：

change 是「零錢」	changes 是「改變」

work 是「工作」	works 是「工程、傑作」
cloth 是「布」	clothes 是「衣服」
paper 是「紙」	papers 是「報紙、論文、試卷」
glass 是「玻璃」	glasses 是「眼鏡」
damage 是「損毀」	damages 是「損害賠償」
time 是「時間」	times 是「時代」
manner 是「方式」	manners「禮貌」
food 是「食物」	foods 是「各類食品」
fruit 是「水果」	fruits 是「各類食品」
fish 是「魚肉」	fishes 是「各種魚類」
chicken 是「雞肉」	chickens 是「各種雞」
staff 是「全體職員」	staffs 是「木棍或各部門的職員」；「一個職員」是 a staff member 或 a member of staff
people 最特別，它沒有 s 卻是複數	peoples 是「各種族的人」

其實，對於句裏的名詞是單數還是複數，我們很多時運用常識就可以。

　　例如：閉上眼睛。

　　　不是 ✘ Close your eye.

　　　而是 ✔ Close your eyes.

除非特別指明，人家叫你閉上眼睛，當然是叫你閉上兩隻眼睛，否則為甚麼只閉上一隻眼睛？

吃飯前要洗手。

　不是 ✘ Wash your hand before you eat.

　而是 ✔ Wash your hands before you eat.

人家叫你洗手，當然是叫你洗兩隻手。為甚麼只洗一隻手？另一隻為甚麼不用洗？

其中一個學生早退。

　不是 ✘ One of the student left early.

　而是 ✔ One of the students left early.

貨車

　不是 ✘ Good vehicle

　而是 ✔ Goods vehicle

1.19 common sense 有助分辨名詞的單複數

上文說過句裏的名詞是單數還是複數，很多時運用常識就可以分辨出來，可能大家還是不大明白，我就以 hand 為例，詳細說明單數名詞和複數名詞的運用。

例如老師對全班同學說「贊成的就舉手」，那用 hand 還是 hands 呢？

那當然是 If you agree, put up your hands. 。

但如果老師只是問一個同學，那自然是 Put up your hand. 。因為叫一個同學 Put up your hands.「舉高兩隻手」有點不妥，對吧？

又例如一個賊人在金飾店持械行劫，他對店內的人說舉高手，應說 Hand up. 還是 Hands up. 呢？那當然是 Hands up. 。

英語有一個慣用語 on the other hand（另一方面），它不是 on the other hands，為甚麼呢？這是因為我們只有兩隻手，除了一隻手之外，我們怎會有 other hands 呢？難道我們還有兩隻或以上的手？

另一個慣用語是「易手、轉手」的英語，應該是 change hand 還是 change hands 呢？當然是 change hands。東西由一方的手轉到另一方的手，自然是多過一隻手，例如：

這房子已幾易其手。

The house has changed <u>hands</u> many times.

「轉火車、轉巴士」呢？當然是複數。例如：

你要在交匯處轉巴士。

You have to change buses at the interchange.

又例如「由可靠的人照顧着、在可靠的人手裏」是 in good <u>hand</u> 還是 in good <u>hands</u> 呢？當然是 in good <u>hands</u>，其他例子還有：

別擔心孩子們 —— 他們由可靠的人照顧着。

不是 ✘ Don't worry about the children – they're in good <u>hand</u>.

而是 ✔ Don't worry about the children – they're in good <u>hands</u>.

因為如果只是由一隻手照顧，怎樣照顧呢？另一隻手休息嗎？

另一常用語 by <u>hand</u> 是「手寫、手工做的或親手遞交」的意思，可以說是 by <u>hands</u> 嗎？

那當然不對，我們用一隻手交給對方不就可以嗎？

其他例子還有：

「第一手、直接地」at first <u>hand</u>

「出自某人之手、因為某人」at someone's <u>hands</u>

「手拉着手、同時發生的」<u>hand</u> in <u>hand</u>

「別碰、不插手」<u>hands</u> off

「洗手不幹」wash one's <u>hands</u> of

說到常識，我們常說的「交友、做朋友」。英語是 make friends 還是 make friend 呢？當然是 make friends，一個人怎樣跟自己「交友、做朋友」呢？

記得中學時代有齣外國電影叫「兩小無猜」，它的英文名稱就是 *Friends*。

1.20 indirect questions 如何避免中式英語結構

由於英語裏的「間接引語」是很普遍的中式英語，所以我在這裏跟大家詳細說明「間接引語」的基本語法規則，讓大家知道怎樣在各式各樣的文件，特別是在會議紀錄裏，避免使用中式英語結構。

首先，大家看看以下錯誤的例子：

他問我們是否同意？

✗ He asked us do you agree?

主席問她為甚麼反對。

✗ The Chairman asked her why did she raise an objection.

陳先生告訴他不要再做。

✗ Mr. Chan told him don't do it again.

她不肯定他們需要甚麼。

✗ She was not sure what did they want.

你知道辦事處現時在哪裏嗎？

✗ Do you know where is the secretariat?

我們現在看看錯誤分析：

✘ He asked us do you agree?

以上是最常見的錯誤。很多同學都不明白甚麼是 indirect questions「間接疑問句」。

首先說「直接疑問句」。當提問者和聽者面對面，並要求聽者給予答覆，則應該使用「直接疑問句」。例如：

"Do you like music?"
"Where are you going?"
"How did you open it?"

至於「間接疑問句」indirect questions，就是把某人提出的「直接疑問句轉述給另一個人，而不需要對方即時答覆。我們會用固定「引述動詞」來引導轉述部份，例如：say、tell 或 ask。

最重要的是必須記住一些「間接疑問句」的規則：轉述「一般疑問句」時，必須用 if 或 whether 來引導被轉述部份；轉述「特殊疑問句」(即含有 what、who、which、why、how 等「特殊疑問詞」的疑問句) 時，必須用以上「特殊疑問詞」來引導被轉述部份；「間接疑問句」不用引號和問號，並且要改變「直接疑問句」的原有詞序和時態等。

正確示例如下：

✔ He asked me if we agreed.

✔ The Chairman asked her why she raised an objection.

和以上例子一樣，我們要對「直接疑問句」作一些改動，使其變為「間接疑問句」，

要刪去問號和「助動詞」did，把「動詞原形」raise 變為「過去時」raised。

✘ Mr. Chan told him don't do it again.

這一句中的 "Don't do it again." 是「直接陳述句」，當 not 轉為「間接陳述句」時不可再用 don't，而要改用「不定式」的否定形式，即「not to + 動詞原形」。

正確示例如下：

✔ Mr. Chan told him not to do it again.

✘ She was not sure what did they want.

這句話的錯誤說明大家不明白「主句」She was not sure... 引導的是一個「間接疑問句」。

大家要記着，「間接疑問句」不單用來轉述別人的問題，還可以用 I wonder、I don't know...、Peter will tell us...、Susan wants to know... 和 I will find out... " 等詞組來引導「直接疑問句」來表示「疑惑」、「好奇」等意思。這類詞組後面的「從句」必須用根據「間接疑問句」的變化規則進行處理。

正確示例如下：

She was not sure what they wanted.

✘ Do you know where is the secretariat?

這一句的特別之處是 Do you know 是「疑問句」形式，它是一個「雙重疑問句」，即在「直接疑問句」中包含「間接疑問句」，需要注意：句末有「問號」，而後半句 Where is the secretariat?，仍要用「間接疑問句」的形式，即用「特殊疑問詞」where 來引導「從句」部份，而且「從句」部份必須採用「陳述句」語序。

正確示例如下：

Do you know where the secretariat is?

如果大家還是不明白，我們現在把相關語法要點重溫一下：

「直接疑問句」分為兩種：「一般疑問句」和「特殊疑問句」，因此要把它們變為「間接疑問句」，可以分成兩種情況：

1 改變「一般疑問句」的規則：

「一般疑問句」是指沒有「特殊疑問詞」(如 who、 where、 why 等)，可以用 yes 和 no 直接作答的疑問句。把這類「直接疑問句」變為「間接疑問句」時，只需用 if 或 whether 來引導轉述內容，轉述內容必須用「陳述句」語序；例如：

直接疑問句：Mr. Wong asked Ms. Lee, "Have you completed your work yet?

間接疑問句：Mr. Wong asked Ms. Lee if / whether she had completed her work yet.

直接疑問句：Mr. Chan asked Mary, "Are you married?"

間接疑問句：Mr. Chan asked Mary if / whether she was married.

2 改變「特殊疑問句」的規則：

    a.「特殊疑問句」指帶「特殊疑問詞」（如 who、where、why 等）、而且不能用 yes 和 no 直接作答的疑問句。

    b. 把「特殊疑問句」改為「間接疑問句」時，注意「從句」必須套用「陳述句」語序，即「動詞」放在「主語」後面。例如：

直接疑問句："What are the men doing?" the officer asked him.
間接疑問句：The officer asked him what the men were doing.

直接疑問句："What's the time?" the Chairman asked.
間接疑問句：The Chairman asked what the time was.
    （並非 ✗ "The Chairman asked what is the time."）

把「陳述句」變為「間接引語」，要注意：

    a. 根據意思，改變敘述中的動詞時態。

直接敘述	間接敘述
一般現在時	一般過去時
現在進行時	過去進行時
現在完成時	過去完成時
現在完成進行時	過去完成進行時
一般過去時	過去完成時
一般將來時	過去將來時

b. 根據意思，改變敘述中的「人稱代名詞」（I、you、he、she、it、they、we 等）、「指示代名詞」（this、that、these、those 等）或所有格形容詞（my、your、his、her、its、our、their 等）。例如：

直接引語：The manager said, "I've given my files to your staff."
間接引語：The manager said he had given his files to our staff.

c. 根據意思，改變敘述的時間副詞或地點副詞。

直接敘述	間接敘述
now	then
today	that day
this morning	that morning
yesterday	the day before / the previous day
yesterday morning	the morning before / the previous morning
last night	the night before / the previous night
last Monday	the Monday before / the previous Monday
ago	before
two days ago	two days before
tomorrow	the next day
next week	the following week
here	there

i) 時間：

> 直接引語："I can't go now," she said. "I'll go tomorrow."
> 間接引語：She said she could not go then. She would go the
> next day.

ii) 地點：

> 直接引語："Put it there, on this desk," I told Wong.
> 間接引語：I told Wong to put it there, on that desk."

! NOTES 注意 !

注意「間接引語」中的指代關係一定要明確，比如，如果用 he 或 she 不能使別人明白 he 或 she 所指是誰，便應該用 he 或 she 的名字。例如：

會話情景：Mary is talking to Susan about her (Mary's) sister.

直接引語：

"She said she lost her ring yesterday when she was swimming with you and me".

間接引語：

Mary told Susan that her (Mary's) sister said that she had lost her ring the previous day when she had been swimming with Susan and Mary.

---

3 如果「直接敘述」的是「祈使句」，那麼改為「間接引語」時要注意：

「主句」的動詞要改用含有祈使意義的詞組，如 tell、ask、request、order 等，「從句」的動詞則應改用「不定式」。例如：

直接引語：The Chairman said to him, "Do not talk nonsense!"
間接引語：The Chairman told him not to talk nonsense.

4 「間接引語」中，出現以下三種情況時，「從句」的「動詞」可以不改時態：

　a. 報告普遍真理。例如：

直接引語：He said, "The sun rises in the east."
間接引語：He said that the sun rises in the east.

　b. 報告歷史事實。例如：

直接引語：She said, "Columbus discovered America."
間接引語：She said that Columbus discovered America.

　c.「直接引語」使用「虛擬語氣」。例如：

直接引語：He said, "I would fly to you at once if I were a bird."
間接引語：He said that he would fly to you at once if he were a bird.

! NOTES 注意 *!*

學習英文「間接疑問句」和「間接引語」時，最重要是要調整語序、人稱和時態。

最重要是中英語序不一定相同。

1.21 沒想到用 kindly 並不客氣

很多人用 Please kindly... 以為這樣更客氣，但其實最好避免使用這種表達方式，因為 kindly 並不是很客氣的說法，可以改作 Please give me a reply.。說 Kindly give me a reply. 不好，因為它含有「你還是……的好，不要違背我的話啊！」的意思，它外表雖然客氣，但實際上有命令性質，會產生誤會或令人反感。以下例子就充滿不耐煩或居高臨下的語氣：

請中午後再致電。

> Kindly call again after noon.

我在看書，請你把收音機的音量調低一點。

> Kindly turn the radio down while I am reading.

請把手挪開。

> Kindly take your hand off.

請把書放好！

> Kindly put that book away!

請告訴我情況為何發展到這種地步？

> Can you kindly tell me how this situation has got this far?

請馬上離開。

> You are kindly requested to leave at once.

請不要打擾我。

> Kindly leave me alone.

其實 kindly 有 please 的意思，所以兩字不需一起使用。

要客客氣氣的説「請」，please 比 kindly 簡單自然。總之，我們提出要求時，可以説 please 的就不要説 kindly。例如：

請告訴我。

Please let me know.

請進來。

Please come in.

如需進一步資料，請與我們聯絡。

Please contact us for further information.

請參閱指引。

Please refer to the guidelines.

除了 kindly 之外，so kind as to 是表達客氣的短語。很多人有時用錯了，錯誤例子如下：

✘ He was presented to the manager, who was so kind to accompany him during his visit.

✔ He was presented to the manager, who was so kind as to accompany him during his visit.

kind enough 也可以表達客氣，上述例句可以改為：

He was presented to the manager, who was kind enough to accompany him during his visit.

1.22 別受中文「出」的影響用錯 out

學習英語的時候，要正確運用介詞 (prepositions) 十分困難，我們除了必須把常用例子寫在筆記簿上，牢牢記着它們之外，還要經常在日常生活加以運用才可以熟能生巧。此外，我們很容易受中文翻譯影響而誤用某些英語介詞。以 <u>out</u> 為例，它不一定要與動詞一起使用來表達中文「出」的意思。像以上「他們講出他們的意見。」*They voiced out their opinions. 是不正確的，句裏的 <u>out</u> 是不需要的。其他錯誤例子還有：

他提出自己真誠的意見。

   ✘ He gave out his honest opinion.

她想講出自己的意見。

   ✘ She likes to express out her opinion.

請指出不同之處。

   ✘ Please spot out the difference.

統計顯示出相同的趨勢。

   ✘ Statistics show out the same trend.

在上述例子，<u>out</u> 是不需要的。現在，我們很多時都不覺得那些 <u>out</u> 是錯誤的，主要原因是我們説中文時有「出」這個字。以下是其他正確例子：

我們表達謝意。

✔ We expressed our thanks.

誰向你發出許可？

✔ Who gave you permission?

他看出一個大錯誤。

✔ He spotted a big mistake.

許多社區道出他們的關注。

✔ Many communities have voiced their concern.

然而，有些動詞單獨使用時通常不需要加 out，它們後面加 out 時會有不同意思。例如：

他們售賣舊傢具。

They sell old furniture.

門票已經售罄。

Tickets were sold out.

這表格列出入職要求。

This form lists the entry requirements.

所有規則在附表裏詳細列明。

All the regulations are listed out in the appendices.

1.23 中英大不同，切勿對號入座

松鼠狗正確的英文名稱是 pomeranian，完全與松鼠無關。為甚麼我在這裏說松鼠狗呢？其實，我想說的是中英翻譯不是中英對譯那麼簡單。關於中英名詞的翻譯，不可能永遠對號入座直譯的。

很多同學以為學英文只要找到相同意思的詞彙便可。換句話說，因為 long 的解釋是「長」，所以 long wave 是「長波」，而「長期服務」的英譯便是 long service，「長征」是 Long March，「長頭髮」是 long hair。但我們也知道 long jump 不是「長跳」而是「跳遠」，long drink 不是「長飲品」而是「高杯飲品」；同樣，「長歎」的英譯不是 long sigh 而是 deep sigh，「長椅」不是 long chair 而是 bench。香港消防處的「長臂猿雲梯車」當然與 long-armed monkey 無關，而是 snorkel。這就是中英翻譯奧妙的地方。

以下是其他錯誤例子及正確翻譯：

1 性病	✘ sex disease	✔ venereal disease
2 熱水爐	✘ hot water stove	✔ water heater
3 抽油煙機	✘ oil and smoke extracting machine	✔ range hood 或 cooker hood
4 防火膠板	✘ fire-proof plastic board	✔ laminate
5 松鼠狗	✘ squirrel dog	✔ pomeranian

6 芝麻斑	✘ sesame grouper	✔ brown-spotted grouper
7 桃駁李	✘ peach-cum-plum	✔ nectarine
8 肥雞丸	✘ fat chicken pill	✔ hexcestrol
9 沙井	✘ sand well	✔ manhole
10 水馬	✘ water horse	✔ zone barrier / water-filled barrier
11 水氣開關	✘ water gas switch	✔ circuit breaker
12 狗仔隊	✘ puppies team	✔ paparazzo / paparazzi
13 造馬案	✘ horse-making case	✔ race-fixing
14 賭外圍	✘ gamble overseas	✔ book-making

最後我想說，即使在互聯網找到相關翻譯，大家都應該找英語參考書或從相關網頁尋找答案加以對照 (cross reference) 和核實英語是否正確，這才是學好英語的最佳方法。

1.24 「沒有令人關注的原因」，不是
There is no reason for concern.

中文裏經常說「理由」及「原因」，但注意英語裏，reason 及 cause 可以是「理由」，也可以是「原因」。首先，cause 是「原因、起因」，指的是造成後果的「原因、起因」。例如：

他被革職的原因是疏忽職守。

The cause for his dismissal was negligence of duty.

暴動/火災有多個原因。

There are many causes to the riot / fire.

控方未能提供拖延的合理原因。

The prosecution has not provided good cause for the delay.

失業是貧窮的主要原因。

Unemployment is the major cause of poverty.

reason 則是人們經過思考分析歸納出來，有關某事發生或做某事的「理由、原因、解釋、道理」。例如：

她說不行，但沒有說明原因。

She said no but she didn't give a reason.

她的理由是探望父親。

Her reason was to visit her father.

請告訴我你遲到這麼久的原因。

Please tell me the <u>reason</u> why you're so late.

因此，大標題的「沒有令人關注的原因。」應改為 There is no <u>cause</u> for concern.。

此外，以下例子用 <u>cause</u> 或 <u>reason</u> 都可以，這主要視乎你想知道甚麼。例如，如果問「延誤的真正原因是甚麼？」，說 What is the actual cause for the delay?，這是想問「為甚麼發生了延誤？」。又例如，問「拖延的理由是甚麼？」，說 What is the reason for the delay?，這是想問「為甚麼要拖延？」。

! NOTES 注意 !

注意中文經常說「原因是因為⋯⋯」，但英文不說 The reason is because...。例如：

原因是因為成本太高。

The <u>reason</u> is that the costs are too high.

更不可以說 Because of this reason, ...。例如：

不是 ✘ Because of this <u>reason</u>, the project was cancelled.

而是 ✔ For this <u>reason</u>, the project was cancelled.

1.25 same 有 the 和沒有 the 含義不同

我們經常說「相同、同樣」，英語是 same ，那是很簡單的英語。但我們很容易忘記 same 的前面應該有 the 或其他指示代詞，在名詞前面只說 same 是錯誤的。例如：

她每天都坐在同一把椅子上。

She sits in the <u>same</u> chair every day.

他們上的是同一所大學。

They went to the <u>same</u> university.

他和我同一天出生。

He was born on the <u>same</u> day as me.

再次抗議的正是那些相同的人。

It was those <u>same</u> people who protested again.

我就站在她 30 年前居住的那所房子前面。

I stood in front of the very <u>same</u> house in which she lived 30 years ago.

大衛說了一模一樣的話。

David said exactly the <u>same</u> thing.

當然，很多人會說為甚麼一定要用 the ，不用 the 大家都會明白 <u>same</u> 的中文意思。其實，英語語法很大部份是規則和習慣用法，都是沒有解釋的。就像 the 一樣，它是 definite article ，

雖然它的使用規則很多，但只要多加運用就可以掌握得到，像太陽 the sun、月亮 the moon 一樣，書本説太陽和月亮在世界裏只有一個，所以要用 the。雖然很多人也會不明白，但只要在實際運用時不要忘記 the 就可以了。

其他例子還有：

他們倆都説同樣的東西。

They both said much the <u>same</u> thing.

他用了相同的字眼。

He used the very <u>same</u> words.

她買了一輛汽車，和我的一模一樣。

She bought the <u>same</u> car as mine.

昨晚我也遇到同樣的事。

The <u>same</u> thing happened to me last night.

但注意在口語：例如説到飲料，以及被人辱罵後作出回應，不加 the 是正確的。

再來一份。

"<u>Same</u> again, please."

"滾！"

"Get lost!"

"<u>Same</u> to you!"

　　"你也滾！"

1.26 sincerely 和 faithfully 不可隨意互換

在一般正式信件裏，我們最常犯的錯誤是把 Yours sincerely 和 Yours faithfully 的用法混淆了。

請記着在英式英語裏，Yours sincerely 通常用於寫信給我們認識的人（並以對方的真實姓名稱呼）作為結束語。Yours faithfully 則用於寫信給我們不認識的人作為結束語。

即是說，當我們寫信稱呼對方為 Dear Mr. Choi 或 Dear Ms. Wong 等，就應該用 Yours sincerely 來結束，不應該用 Yours faithfully。

當我們寫信稱呼對方為 Dear Sir 或 Dear Madam 等，就應該用 Yours faithfully 來結束，不用 Yours sincerely。

因此，在一般商業信件裏，我們說 Dear Customer 或 Dear Valued Customer 時，都應該用 Yours faithfully。

Yours faithfully 在英國比美國普通。

在美式英語裏，一般用 Sincerely yours、Sincerely 或 Yours truly。

Yours truly 省去 yours 會令語氣更隨便。

希望大家知道上述區別後，以後寫英文信就不會混淆 Yours sincerely 和 Yours faithfully。

1.27 中文「建議去做」不要説 suggest to

在日常生活及一般文件裏，suggest 很常見，解作「提議、建議」，它是動詞，但經常有人混淆它的用法，以下是錯誤例子：

我們建議他停止。

✘ We suggested him to stop.

他建議她早一點離開。

✘ He suggested her to leave early.

議員提議有關部門作出改善。

✘ Members suggested the department concerned to make improvements.

主席提議會議繼續十五分鐘。

✘ The Chairman suggested that the meeting continued for 15 minutes.

她建議下午一時吃午餐。

✘ She suggested to have lunch at 1 p.m.

上述各句受了中文「建議或提議某人去做某事」的句式影響，因而在 suggested 後面出現「不定式 to」或「過去時」，那是不對的。

請記着：在 suggest 後面，我們應用 that 子句，並可加上 might 或 should。我們加上動名詞也可以。所以上述各句應改為：

✔ We <u>suggested</u> that he should stop.

✔ He <u>suggested</u> that she should leave early.

✔ Members <u>suggested</u> that the department concerned should make improvements.

✔ The Chairman <u>suggested</u> that the meeting should continue for 15 minutes.

✔ She <u>suggested</u> having lunch at 1 p.m.

請注意很多時候，<u>suggested</u> 後面的 that 和 should 可以不用寫出來。其他例子還有：

主席建議我們讓他們繼續進行。

The Chairman <u>suggested</u> that we let them proceed.

他提議用其他方式做這事。

He <u>suggested</u> doing it a different way.

我建議你三思而後行。

May I <u>suggest</u> that you think carefully.

1.28 「更新」不一定用 update

我們學習英語詞彙和翻譯時，最大的問題是經常對號入座。現時網上或其他電腦翻譯，因使用配對 (matching) 的方法而出現錯誤。以 update 為例，由於近數十年來科技進步，我們經常說「更新」和 update。但大家要注意，雖然 update 是「更新」的意思，但「更新」不一定是 update。 請大家看看以下錯誤例子：

更新伙伴關係

　　✘ update partnerships

課程更新

　　✘ curriculum update

更新通知

　　✘ update notice

以上英語就是中式英語，因為英文沒有 update partnerships、curriculum update 和 update notice 的說法。正確的英語如下：

　　✔ renew partnerships
　　✔ curriculum renewal
　　✔ renewal notice

事實上，「更新」除了 update，還可以是 renew、 upgrade、regenerate、 renovate 和 replace the old with new。例如：

會籍必須每年更新一次。

Membership must be renewed annually.

更新成本

Replacement cost

更新儲備金

Replacement reserve

英文 update 的正確使用例子如下：

存摺已經更新。

The passbook has been <u>updated</u>.

我們的記錄定期更新。

Our records are regularly <u>updated</u>.

1.29 works 不是工作

*Finish all your works. 這一句錯在 works，因為 work 解作工作的時候，它是不可數名詞，而它像其他常見的不可數名詞如 furniture、equipment、luggage、water、information 等一樣，永遠是單數形式的。至於 works，它是「工程、工務、工事或藝術、小說、文學作品／傑作」的意思，因此應改為 Finish all your work.

更多解釋

1. 對於名詞，我們首先需要知道名詞可分為可數名詞和不可數名詞。

我們可以數到一些物件或東西例如 table、car、tree 和 angle，所以它們叫可數名詞，它可以和數字 one、two、three 等以及冠詞（Articles）—— a 和 an 連用，並有複數形式。

我們數不到 jealousy、dust 和 smoke，所以它們叫不可數名詞或物質名詞（Material Nouns）。它作為沒有清楚界限的物質，而且不能作為單個物件看待的物品、液體、抽象品質、收藏物和其他東西的名稱。這些名詞許多永遠是單數形式，大多數沒有複數形式。

2. 我們必須緊記可數名詞和不可數名詞前面的正確用詞，例如：

可數名詞		不可數名詞	
(not) many	cars	(not) much	dirt
a few	girls	a little	rice
some	bottles	some	cheese
(not) a lot of	books	(not) a lot of	water
a number of	reasons	an amount of	butter
		a quantity of	petrol

some 和 (not) a lot of 最有用，因為兩者都可以用於可數名詞和不可數名詞。

1. 同樣，我們也必須記住，在不可數名詞或可數名詞後面，動詞（Verbs）必須分別作出相應的配合，以便名詞與動詞有一致性（Agreement）。例如：

These books are mine. (因為 books 是複數，所以後面用 are。)

The boys have left. (因為 boys 是複數，所以後面用 have。)

The girls are swimming. (因為 girls 是複數，所以後面用 are。)

The cars were damaged. (因為 cats 是複數，所以後面用 were。)

The money is hers. (因為 money 是單數，所以後面用 is。)

The rain has just come on. (因為 rain 是單數，所以後面用 has。)

The roof was leaking. (因為 roof 是單數，所以後面用 was。)

The only trouble is the plan won't work. (因為 trouble 是單數，所以後面用 is。)

2. 通常不可數名詞永遠是單數形式的，下表為某些例子：

aircraft	alcohol	attention	bait	blame	blood
bread	change*	clothing	conduct	corn	damage*
dirt	dust	education	equipment	evidence	excitement
fighting	firework	food	for example	fruit	fun
furniture	garbage	grass	hair	homework	housework
information	knowledge	land	laughter	luggage	machinery
money	mud	music	news*	nonsense	paper*
people**	prey	progress	property	rainfall	scenery
shouting	slang	smoke	social work	staff**	stationery
sweat	the following	thunder	toast	traffic	training
trouble	work*				

請留心一些名詞既可用作不可數名詞，又可用作可數名詞，主要是意思有所不同 *。

Change* 解作零錢時，它是不可數名詞；
Changes 指許多改變、變更、變化。

Paper* 解作紙張時，它是不可數名詞；
Papers 指多份報紙、論文、考卷。

Damage* 解作損害、破壞、破損時，它是不可數名詞；
Damages 指賠償、損害賠償，它是單數，複數形式不變。

Work* 解作工作時，它是不可數名詞；   Works 指工程、傑作、作品，它是單數，複數形式不變。
News* 解作新聞時，它是單數，複數形式不變。
People** 是單數形式但含複數意義，單數形式是 Person；   Peoples 指不同種族的人。
Staff** 是單數，也是複數。   Staffs 解作木棍、木棒、不同部門的員工。   為避免錯誤，我們說員工時可以改說 member(s) of staff / staff member(s)

要了解某個名詞是否可數名詞及它的確切用法，我們應查閱詞典。通常，在詞典裏可數名詞是用 C 表示的；不可數名詞是用 U 表示的。

5. 不可數名詞的量詞

1. 對於不可數名詞或物質名詞，我們必須明白它是沒有清楚界限的物質，因此不能作為單個物件看待的物品、液體、抽象品質、收藏物和其他東西的名稱。我們常常在它的前面用了 a，例如 *a soap、*a bread、*a gold、*a milk 等就是典型的錯誤。

為了避免這些錯誤，我們應該用適當的量詞（Quantifier）配合，如 a piece of 或數量很少可以用 a bit of，說一些則用 some pieces 或 bits of。

常見的正確例子：

I would like a piece / bit of cake / bread.
我想要一塊 / 一點兒蛋糕 / 麵包。

Please give me some pieces of / bits of paper / wood.
請給我幾片 / 幾塊紙 / 木頭。

She needs a piece of chalk / meat.
她要一支粉筆 / 一片肉。

a bar of soap / chocolate / gold / steel
一塊肥皂 / 巧克力 / 黃金 / 鋼鐵

a drop of water / blood / oil / vinegar / milk / petrol
一滴水 / 血 / 油 / 醋 / 牛奶 / 電油

a loaf of bread
一條麵包
　（bread 是「枕頭包」，我們說一個一個的麵包是 bun，例如叉燒包是 BBQ-pork bun）

a slice of bread / cucumber / meat / pineapple
一片麵包 / 黃瓜 / 肉 / 菠蘿

a lump of dough / mud / clay / sugar / coal
一塊麵粉團 / 泥團 / 陶土 / 方糖 / 煤
　（lump 即一塊、一粒）

a grain of sand / salt / rice / corn
一粒沙 / 鹽 / 大米 / 玉米

a sack of rice / cement / paper
一袋大米 / 水泥 / 紙

a sheet of paper / metal / plastic 一張紙 / 金屬板 / 一塊塑料
a sheet / pane of glass 一塊 / 一片玻璃
a reel of cotton / thread 一捲棉花 / 線
a roll of cloth 一捲布

請留心，一條 / 一塊巧克力是 "a bar / piece of chocolate"、巧克力蛋糕是 "a chocolate cake"、巧克力製造廠是 "a chocolate factory"。

當它是巧克力糖、夾心巧克力糖時，便是可數名詞，例如：

我買了一盒巧克力糖。

I have bought a box of chocolates.

2. 永遠是複數形式的詞語是不可以沒有 "s" 的，下表為某些例子：

barracks	billiards	clothes*	congratulations
crossroads	headquarters	glasses*	goods
jeans	mathematics	manners*	means
nowadays	proceeds	pajamas	scissors
series	species	spirits	surroundings
Swiss	times*	trousers	

請留心，一些複數形式的名詞亦有單數形式，主要是意思有所不同 *。

clothes* 解作衣服時，它沒有單數的形式；cloth 是布。
glasses* 解作眼鏡；glass 是玻璃、玻璃杯。
manners* 解作禮貌；manner 是方式、態度。
times* 解作時代；time 是時間。

1.30 表達「有利」時,用 favourable to 還是 in favour of?

我們經常說「有利」,在商業文件裏,使用簡單實用的英文是 <u>favourable</u>。例如:

有利的經濟環境

✔ <u>favourable</u> economic conditions

天氣仍然對我們有利。

✔ The weather is still <u>favourable</u> to us.

它也是「讚賞、同意、很好」的意思。例如:

讚賞的評論文章 / 反應

✔ <u>favourable</u> reviews / reactions

他的請求得到同意。

✔ His request met with a <u>favourable</u> response.

很好的印象

✔ <u>favourable</u> impression

好評

✔ <u>favourable</u> comments

<u>favourable</u> 也是「贊成」的意思,等於 <u>in favour of</u>,但必須用

「人」作為主語。例如：

大多數人都贊成這個主意。

✔ Most people are <u>favourable</u> to the idea.

他贊成我們的計劃。

✔ He is <u>favourable</u> to our plan.

他們贊成他的建議。

✔ They are <u>in favour of</u> his suggestion.

大部份回應者贊成廢除這種分別。

✔ The majority of respondents were <u>in favour of</u> the abolition of that distinction.

下列是錯誤的例子：

協議條款對我們有利。

不是 ✘ The terms of the agreement are <u>in favour of</u> us.

而是 ✔ The terms of the agreement are <u>favourable</u> to us.

1.31 favourite 之前不能加 most，為甚麼？

我們申請職位獲邀參加面試時，經常會自我介紹，並且講到自己的嗜好及最喜愛的運動，例如「蘋果是我最喜愛的水果。」Apple is my *most <u>favourite</u> fruit.；「網球是我最喜愛的運動。」Tennis is my *most <u>favourite</u> sport.，但說 *most <u>favourite</u> 是不對的。為甚麼呢？這是因為 <u>favourite</u> 是形容詞，它已包含「最喜愛」的意思，我們不應再用 most ✘ 來修飾。現在就讓我們看看 <u>favourite</u> 的常見例子：

這是我最喜愛的電影之一。

It's one of my <u>favourite</u> movies.

誰是你最喜愛的歌星？

Who is your <u>favourite</u> singer?

二月是我最喜愛的月份。

February is my <u>favourite</u> month.

你最喜愛甚麼電視節目？

What is your <u>favourite</u> television programme?

<u>favourite</u> 也是名詞，它是「最喜愛的人或事物」的意思。例如：

女士們最喜愛這種手袋。

These handbags are great <u>favourites</u> with the ladies.

你最喜愛哪一個？

Which one is your <u>favourite</u>?

他的歌我全都喜歡，但這首是我最喜愛的。

I like all his songs but this one is my <u>favourite</u>.

當老師的不應該在班上有最喜愛的學生。

A teacher should not have <u>favourites</u> in the class.

他是選舉裏最有希望勝出的人。

He is the <u>favourite</u> to win in the election.

在賽馬裏，<u>favourite</u> 是「熱門馬」的意思，hot <u>favourite</u> 就是「大熱門」。

1.32 稱讚別人優雅，用 graceful 還是 gracious？

很多人經常混淆 <u>graceful</u> 和 <u>gracious</u>，以為兩者都是「優雅」的意思。但只要我們仔細看一看它們的英文意思，就知道兩者是不同的。<u>graceful</u> 是 moving in a smooth and attractive way 或是 having a smooth and attractive shape，即是「優美、優雅、優良」的意思，它形容動作姿態優美動人。<u>gracious</u> 是 comfortable and with a good appearance and quality，即「和藹可親、謙恭、慈祥」的意思，它一般用於表示人本身的禮貌，通常指地位高貴的人彬彬有禮。例如：

優美的書法

a <u>graceful</u> writing

她身材高大，動作優美。

She was tall and <u>graceful</u>.

她優雅地向觀眾鞠了一躬。

She gave a <u>graceful</u> bow to the audience.

沒有跟她說「不可以」的優雅方式。

There was no <u>graceful</u> way to tell her "no".

她們的舞姿優雅。

Their dancing was <u>graceful</u>.

他最後道了歉，但風度不夠。

He finally apologised, but he was not very <u>graceful</u> about it.

慈祥的微笑

A <u>gracious</u> smile

這種優裕的生活不適合他；他寧願過簡樸的生活。

All this <u>gracious</u> living is not for him; he prefers the simple life.

她對所有客人都和藹可親。

She was <u>gracious</u> to all her guests.

還有更多例子：

建立綠色學校，就能夠保留優良的耕種傳統。

不是 ✘ Building a green school can sustain the <u>gracious</u> farming traditions.

而是 ✔ Building a green school can sustain the <u>graceful</u> farming traditions.

他是一個非常和藹可親的人，他的意見指導我在日本的生活。

不是 ✘ He was a very <u>graceful</u> human being, whose advice guided me during my time in Japan.

而是 ✔ He was a very <u>gracious</u> human being, whose advice guided me during my time in Japan.

1.33 「租屋」、「租船」、「租車」該用 hire 還是 rent？

在日常生活裏，無論因工作或外遊而說到「租用」或「僱用 / 聘請」，經常會用 <u>hire</u>，但也經常用得不正確。例如：

他在倫敦的時候，租了一輛汽車用了一個星期。

> 不是 ✘ He <u>rented</u> a car for a week when he was in London.

> 而是 ✔ He <u>hired</u> a car for a week when he was in London.

為甚麼呢？這主要是英式英語及美式英語的問題，我們生活在以英式英語為主的香港，必須小心使用 <u>hire</u>。在英式英語裏，短期租用東西時應該說 <u>hire</u>，我們出租東西會說 <u>hire</u> out。例如：

讓我們去租一輛汽車度週末。

> Let's <u>hire</u> a car for the weekend.

他必須為婚禮租一套禮服。

> He will have to <u>hire</u> a suit for the wedding.

長期租用東西時應該說 <u>rent</u>。例如：

他們租了一台彩色電視機。

> They <u>rented</u> a colour television.

其實，<u>rent</u> 在英國通常只用於房屋及土地，<u>rent</u> a house or a

flat，出租房屋用 let (out)。但在美國，物主出租所有東西都用 <u>rent</u> out。

另一方面，在美式英語中，「僱用」或「聘請」用 hire。

他兩年前在紐約獲得聘用。

He was <u>hired</u> in New York two years ago.

但在英式英語裏，只為某種用途而非長期僱用才用 hire，否則用 appoint，即「聘用」或「任用」。例如：

聘請律師

<u>hire</u> a lawyer

我們僱用一家廣告代理來推銷我們的新產品。

We <u>hired</u> an advertising agent to help sell our new product.

他們準備聘請一名新的生物老師。

They are going to appoint a new biology teacher.

其他例子還有：

有小船出租

boats for <u>hire</u>

付房間的租金

To pay for the <u>hire</u> of a room

1.34 開不起玩笑不是 can't accept a joke

我們經常說「講笑、開玩笑」，它的英語是 a <u>joke</u> 或 <u>jokes</u>。但「講笑、開玩笑」不是 *saying a <u>joke</u> 或 <u>jokes</u>，所以「他們總是對他的小狗開玩笑。」不是 *They are always saying <u>jokes</u> about his dog.、「他總是講笑。」也不是 *He is always saying <u>jokes</u>.。讓我們先看看正確例子：

他本意講笑，但她對他認真。

✔ He meant it as a <u>joke</u>, but she took him seriously.

她就是開不起玩笑。

✔ She just can't take a <u>joke</u>.

我不明白 / 理解那笑話。

✔ I didn't get / understand the <u>joke</u>.

那測試是個笑話。

✔ That test was a <u>joke</u>.

在樹林迷路不是開玩笑。

✔ Being lost in the woods is no <u>joke</u>.

因此，第一段裏兩個錯誤應分別改為：

✔ They are always making <u>jokes</u> about his dog.

✔ He is always telling <u>jokes</u>.

其他正確例子還有：

她開了一些有趣的玩笑。

✔ She told / made some funny <u>jokes</u>.

他站起來時，照例又開起了玩笑。

When he stood up, he made his usual <u>jokes</u>.

他對他們講鴨子過馬路的笑話。

He told them the <u>joke</u> about the ducks crossing the road.

barracks	billiards	<u>clothes*</u>	congratulations
crossroads	headquarters	<u>glasses*</u>	goods
jeans	mathematics	<u>manners*</u>	means
nowadays	proceeds	pajamas	scissors
series	species	spirits	surroundings
Swiss	<u>times*</u>	trousers	

! NOTES 注意 !

Joke 也是動詞。例如：
他們在職員面前從不拿總經理的事來開玩笑。
They never <u>joked</u> about the general manager in front of the staff.

別擔心，他只是開玩笑。
Don't worry, he <u>was</u> only <u>joking</u>.

1.35 行李超過一件時，如何用 luggage 表達？

luggage 是集體名詞，指行李或旅行袋、旅行箱、手提包等。這是不可數名詞，沒有複數，美國人愛用 baggage，也同樣總是以單數形式出現。中文經常說「你有很多件行李。」，有些人受到中文影響，就會說 *You have many luggages. 但這是錯誤的。有關名詞的單複數區別，請參考 works 那一章。以下是 luggage 的錯誤例子：

把行李放在手推車上。

✘ Put your luggages on the trolley.

還有地方再放更多行李。

✘ There is room for more luggages.

請看管着行李，我去找計程車。

✘ Stay with the luggages when I find a taxi.

我在等我的行李。

✘ I am waiting for my luggages.

那車塞滿了太多行李。

✘ The car was overloaded with luggages.

上述例子使用複數是不對的，應該用單數。

「你有很多件行李。」應改為 You have much luggage.。

其他正確例子還有：

千萬別忽略你的行李。

✔ Never leave your luggage unattended.

為甚麼要帶這麼多行李？

✔ Why do you have so much luggage?

把你的手提行李放在輸送帶上。

✔ Place your hand luggage on to the conveyor belt.

! NOTES 注意 *!*

行李架是 luggage rack；行李標籤 / 牌是 luggage label / tag。

1.36 借書到期、合約到期究竟用 overdue 還是 expire？

我們經常說「過期、到期、期滿」，英文是 expire，但很多時我們經常把它和 <u>overdue</u> 混淆了。以下是錯誤例子：

兩國之間的貿易協定將於明年到期。

✘ The trade agreement between the two countries will be <u>overdue</u> next year.

他的駕駛執照已過期。

✘ His driving licence has been <u>overdue</u>.

租約 1987 年到期。

✘ The lease was <u>overdue</u> in 1987.

她的護照上月到期。

✘ Her passport was <u>overdue</u> last month.

那電腦在保證書到期後失靈。

✘ The computer was out of order after the guarantee had been <u>overdue</u>.

在以上例子裏，我們不該使用 <u>overdue</u>，因為 <u>overdue</u> 是表示「賬單到期未付、借的書到期未還或火車和飛機晚點」的意思，它是形容詞。

表示「合同、協議或執照期滿」應該用 expire，它是動詞。

其他 overdue 的正確例子還有：

這書已過期四天。

　　✔ The book is four days <u>overdue</u>.

煤氣單已過期。

　　✔ The gas bill was <u>overdue</u>.

飛機晚點幾小時。

　　✔ The aircraft is <u>overdue</u> by several hours.

現在房租已到期。

　　✔ The rent is now <u>overdue</u>.

! NOTES 注意 *!*

由於 expire 是動詞，不是形容詞，它的前面是不需要加 be 動詞的。詳見 expire 一章。

1.37 well received 原來與「收到」無關

很多時候，我們在收到電子郵件後，都會習慣地寫上 Well received with thanks，以表示已讀，更是「收妥並感謝」的意思。但其實 Well received 的意思是某事物獲得良好反應、普遍接受、歡迎及好評，與收到無關。例如：

這齣電影／本書／報告受到好評。

This film / book / report is <u>well received</u>.

該決定得到了大眾的普遍接受。

The decision was <u>well received</u> by the community.

他們的努力獲得認可。

Their efforts were <u>well-received</u>.

職員對新設備的接受程度非常高。

The new devices have been <u>well received</u> by the staff.

我們想表達收到電郵，正確寫法如下：

收到電郵，感謝。

Received with thanks.

知悉了。

Well noted.

已知，感謝來郵。

Noted with thanks.

其他配合 well 使用的常用形容詞例子：

座無虛席的會議

A well-attended conference

均衡的飲食

A well-balanced diet

觀眾很守秩序。

The audience was well behaved.

她寫的書很有名。

Her books are well-known.

他的牛排全熟。

His steak is well done.

介詞混淆

21 與 guarantee 搭配要用哪個介詞才正確？

在日常生活、商業活動或文件裏,「擔保、保證」的英文是 guarantee,它很常用,是動詞也是名詞。例如「保證書」是 certificate of guarantee 或 guarantee certificate。

它用作動詞的例子:

製造商對這手錶保用五年。

The manufacturers <u>guarantee</u> the watch for five years.

他們保證在兩天之內交貨。

They have <u>guaranteed</u> delivery within two days.

這張票可保證你免費入場。

The ticket will <u>guarantee</u> you free entry.

這冰箱保用四年。

This refrigerator is <u>guaranteed</u> for four years.

保用有效兩年。

The <u>guarantee</u> lasts for two years.

它用作名詞的例子:

這手提電腦出售,如有重大缺陷可保用兩年。

The laptop is sold with a two-year <u>guarantee</u> against major defects.

這洗衣機附有保用。

The washing machine comes with a <u>guarantee</u>.

這冷氣機有三年的保用期。

The air-conditioner has a three-year <u>guarantee</u>.

無法保證商議將可達成協議。

There was no <u>guarantee</u> that the discussions will lead to a deal.

我們要說保用之中是 <u>under guarantee</u>，等於 <u>under warranty</u>。但留意以下例子：

這輛車還在保用之中。

不是 ✘ The car is still *in guarantee.

而是 ✔ The car is still <u>under guarantee</u>.

這手提電腦只買了一年，還在保用之中。

不是 ✘ The laptop is only one year old and is still *in guarantee.

而是 ✔ The laptop is only one year old and is still <u>under guarantee</u>.

22 incapable 不可搭配 to

日前看到聯合國一篇關於國家法院的文章，有這麼一句 "except ... in cases where it is clear that a national judiciary is incapable or unwilling to conduct fair and credible legal proceedings"，句裏 <u>incapable</u> 用得不正確，應改用 unable。這是因為談及有沒有能力，會不會做某事時，除了用形容詞 able to 和 unable to 之外，還可以用 capable 和 <u>incapable</u>，但我們必須留意 capable 和 <u>incapable</u> 後面要用 of 而不是 to。因此，以下 <u>incapable</u> 的例子是錯誤的：

他們不能靠自己工作。

✘ They are <u>incapable</u> to work by themselves.

她不能明白簡單的指示。

✘ She is <u>incapable</u> to understand simple instructions.

他們不會欺騙你。

✘ They are <u>incapable</u> to deceive you.

他當時沒有能力控制好他的車。

✘ He was <u>incapable</u> to have proper control of his car.

上述例子應改為：

✔ They are <u>incapable of</u> working by themselves.

✔ She is <u>incapable of</u> understanding simple instructions.

✔ They are <u>incapable of</u> deceiving you.

✔ He was <u>incapable of</u> having proper control of his car.

其他正確例子還有：

他們沒有能力履行合同條款。

✔ They were <u>incapable of</u> fulfilling the terms and conditions of the contract.

兒童在法律上被視為無能力犯罪。

✔ A child is considered legally <u>incapable of</u> committing a crime.

公司沒有能力實施任何計劃。

✔ The company is <u>incapable of</u> putting any plan into effect.

這輛舊車開不到很高速。

✔ The old car is <u>incapable of</u> reaching very high speed.

23 inferior 須搭配 to

在英語裏，我們比較兩個人或事物之差異時，經常用 "... than" 來表示。例如 "taller than、shorter than、bigger than、smaller than、more beautiful than、more exciting than、more useful than、better than、worse than"。但當我們用 inferior 來表示「……差或不如」時，必須注意它後面是用 to 而不是 than。以下是錯誤例子：

他感到比她差。

> ✘ He felt inferior than her.

這些蘋果 (質量上) 比那些差。

> ✘ These apples (in quality) are inferior than those.

她的工作比他的差。

> ✘ Her work is inferior than his.

現代音樂經常讓人覺得是比過去的差。

> ✘ Modern music is often considered inferior than that of the past.

他們感到低人一等。

> ✘ They felt inferior than the others.

在上述例子，我們應改用 "inferior to"。

其他正確例子還有：

他們數目上比整體人口少。

They are numerically <u>inferior</u> to the rest of the population.

他們看不起她，認為她比他差。

They had looked down on her as being <u>inferior</u> to him.

那些存貨在亞洲市場以較低價出售。

The stocks were sold at prices <u>inferior</u> to Asian market.

! NOTES 注意 *!*

inferior goods / products 是品質較差的貨品 / 產品，即次貨。

inferior court 是下級法庭，而 inferiority complex 是自卑感。

24 intrude 作為不及物動詞時不可直接用名詞

近年社會十分關注如何杜絕侵犯個人私隱的行為,「侵犯」的英語是 intrude ,它是「入侵、侵擾、打擾」的意思。注意「侵犯個人資料私隱」不是 intrude personal data privacy。「侵擾該人對私隱的合理期望」也不是 intrude his reasonable expectation of privacy。為甚麼呢?

因為 intrude 解作「入侵、侵擾、打擾」時是不及物動詞 (intransitive verb),它後面不能直接用名詞,應該用介詞 into、on 或 upon。例如:

我不想打擾你。

I don't want to intrude on you.

他們干涉了令她傷心的私事。

They have intruded upon her private grief.

記者經常侵犯她的私人生活。

Reporters constantly intruded into her private life.

電話聲把他從夢中吵醒了。

The sound of the telephone intruded into his dreams.

公園會影響本區的生活方式。

A park would intrude on the local way of life.

請勿侵犯個人私隱。

Please do not intrude into personal data privacy.

他們侵擾了他對私隱的合理期望。

They have intruded into his reasonable expectation of privacy.

它的名詞是 intrusion。例如：

他們的問題干涉他的私生活。

Their questions are an intrusion on his privacy.

新機場的噪音侵擾了他們的生活。

The noise from the new airport is an intrusion on their lives.

她對外部世界的侵擾感到憤慨。

She resents the intrusion of the outside world.

25 別混淆 age 和 at、in 或 of 的不同搭配

在香港，尋找工作是日常生活的一部份。我們到機構面試時，無可避免會用英語作自我介紹。但很可惜，很多人表達自己的年紀時經常出錯。例如說「我今年二十歲。」，以下都是錯誤例子：

 ✘ I am twenty of <u>age</u>.

 ✘ My <u>age</u> is twenty years old.

 ✘ I am <u>aged</u> twenty years old.

「我今年二十歲。」最簡單的英文是 I am twenty years old. 或 I am twenty.

另外，以下各句意思相同：

 I am twenty years of <u>age</u>.

 I am <u>aged</u> twenty.

 My <u>age</u> is twenty.

 My <u>age</u> is twenty years.

 I am <u>aged</u> twenty years.

至於 I am <u>aged</u> twenty years. 有時可能是「在容貌或精神方面好像老了二十年」的意思。

! *NOTES* 注意 !

<u>age</u> 前面可以用 at、in 或 of，但意思不同：She died at the <u>age</u> of eighty. 裏的 <u>age</u> 指「年齡」，She died in her old <u>age</u>. 裏的 <u>age</u> 是指「人生的一段時間」，She died in an <u>age</u> of social unrest. 裏的 <u>age</u> 是指「時代」，She is of my <u>age</u>. 是「她跟我同年。」的意思。

26 分辨 agree 和 to、with 或 on 的 搭配用法

大家對 agree 應該不會陌生，它是動詞，可解作「贊成、贊同、同意或商定」。但用得不小心就會出錯。例如：

他同意他們的看法。

✘ He <u>agreed to</u> them.

✔ He <u>agreed with</u> them.

我希望他們完全同意所有事情。

✘ I hope they <u>agree with</u> everything.

✔ I hope they <u>agree on</u> everything.

委員會決不贊成我們的市場推廣計劃。

✘ The Committee would never <u>agree on</u> our marketing plan.

✔ The Committee would never <u>agree with</u> our marketing plan.

他同意他們對形勢的分析。

✘ He <u>agreed to</u> their analysis of the situation.

✔ He <u>agreed with</u> their analysis of the situation.

> # ! *NOTES* 注意 !
>
> 惟獨有決定權的人才可以用 <u>agree to</u> ，即「贊成」或「同意」。

此外，當 <u>agree to</u> 用於 suggestion 、 proposal 或 plan 之前，它和 accept 同義。例如：

你認為他們會接受我的建議嗎？

✔ Do you think they will <u>agree to</u> / accept my suggestions?

其他 <u>agree</u> 的正確例子還有：

我們在這問題上看法一致嗎？

✔ Do we all <u>agree on</u> this?

我非常同意你的觀點 / 他們的建議。

✔ I very much <u>agree to</u> your point / their proposal.

他完全同意她講的話。

✔ He <u>agreed</u> entirely <u>with</u> everything she had said.

這個計劃行得通，你同意嗎？

✔ Do you <u>agree with</u> me that the plan will work?

我們商定下次開會日期。

✔ We <u>agreed on</u> the date of next meeting.

27 「安排」該用 arrange to 還是 arrange for？

各類日常公文或文件裏，經常出現「安排」，很多時候它會被翻譯為 arrange，可惜很多人使用 arrange 時，錯誤在它後面直接加賓語及不定式 to，以下是常見的錯誤例子：

請安排他們使用半天服務。

✘ Please <u>arrange</u> them to receive half-day services.

安排他們訪問不同機構。

✘ <u>Arrange</u> them to visit different organisations.

安排會員進行監察工作。

✘ <u>Arrange</u> its members to perform the monitoring work.

請安排他們出席培訓課程。

✘ Please <u>arrange</u> them to attend training courses.

在上述例子裏，arrange 後面應該加上介詞 for 才正確。其他例子還有：

你可以安排一輛計程車在車站接我嗎？

✔ Can you <u>arrange</u> for a taxi to pick me up from the station?

遠遊之前我們已安排好狗兒由朋友照顧。

✔ We <u>arranged</u> for the dogs to stay with our friends while we were away.

她安排好兒子上游泳課。

✓ She <u>arranged</u> for her son to have swimming lessons.

其實，<u>arrange</u> 經常與介詞 for 連用。例如：

會議已安排在星期三舉行。

✓ The meeting has been <u>arranged</u> for Wednesday.

讓我們嘗試為瑪麗安排生日派對。

✓ Let's try to <u>arrange</u> a party for Mary's birthday.

我們已安排了一輛貨車。

✓ We have <u>arranged</u> for a lorry.

28 complain 何時後跟 about？

近年來，香港社會非常盛行投訴文化。為了尋求公義或維護個人利益，不少人經常會投訴。投訴的英文是 <u>complain</u>，它是動詞，名詞是 <u>complaint</u>。

很可惜，有些投訴人除了發音不正確（誤讀為 com plan 或 com pan）之外，運用動詞 <u>complain</u> 也會出錯。錯誤例子如下：

我要投訴那售貨員。

✘ I want to <u>complain</u> the salesman.

那顧客投訴巴士服務。

✘ The customer <u>complained</u> the bus service.

很多人投訴噪音。

✘ Lots of people <u>have complained</u> the noise.

他們總是投訴電視節目裏有太多暴力。

✘ They <u>are complaining</u> all the violence on television.

上述句子錯在甚麼地方呢？原來是句裏 complain 後面若有賓語時，則必須用介詞 about。

像上述各例都需要在 <u>complain / complained</u> 後面加上 about。

總之，我們說投訴某人或物時，英文必須說 <u>complain</u> about。

其他例子還有：

成千上萬的電視觀眾投訴那節目。

✔ Over thousands of viewers <u>complained</u> about the programme.

他們老是投訴鄰居。

✔ They <u>were</u> always <u>complaining</u> about their neighbours.

人總是投訴缺乏解釋。

✔ People always <u>complain</u> about lack of explanation.

! NOTES 注意 *!*

如果我們說向某人、機構或部門投訴時，介詞不是用 about，應用 to。例如：

你應向經理 / 警方 / 消費者委員會投訴。

✔ You should <u>complain</u> to the manager / police / Consumer Council.

不用賓語的 <u>complain</u> 是「抱怨、訴苦」的意思。例如：她總是怨天尤人。

✔ She <u>is</u> always <u>complaining</u>.

29 concern 不一定後跟 for，小心別混淆

許多機構經常會用 <u>concern</u> 來表示關注某事或情況，但有時會混淆它的名詞或動詞用法，因而出現錯誤。例如：

他們對該情況表示深切關注。

不是 ✗ They deeply <u>concern</u> for the situation.

而是 ✓ They <u>are</u> deeply <u>concerned</u> for the situation.

我們對此問題深表關注。

不是 ✗ We serious <u>concern</u> about the problem.

而是 ✓ We have / express serious <u>concern</u> about the problem.

! NOTES 注意 *!*

<u>concern</u> 用作動詞時，只用 <u>concern</u> 是錯誤的，需用助動詞加過去分詞（past participle）。

<u>concern</u> 是「關注、關心」的意思，它是名詞。例如：

失業問題是他們主要關注的事。

✓ Unemployment is their main <u>concern</u>.

近來罪案上升是公眾極為關注的事。

✓ The recent rise in crime is a matter of public <u>concern</u>.

我們關注的是治療的副作用。

✔ The <u>concern</u> that we have is the side effects of the treatment.

<u>concern</u> 也是「擔心、憂慮」的意思。例如：

沒有要擔心的理由。

✔ There is no cause for <u>concern</u>.

會議上，他們提出對環境衛生情況的關注。

✔ In the meeting, they raised <u>concerns</u> about environmental hygiene.

<u>concern</u> 要加上 be 動詞和變成過去分詞才是「關心」的意思。例如：

我們很關心如何讓所有職員知道最新消息。

✔ We <u>were</u> very <u>concerned</u> to keep the staff informed.

他們更關心的是權力和控制而不是居民利益。

✔ They <u>are</u> more <u>concerned</u> with power and control than with the good of the residents.

她真心關心貧民。

✔ She <u>was</u> really <u>concerned</u> for the poor.

2*10* consider 不可單獨搭配不定式 to

大家在職業生涯裏，可能曾因為遇到不愉快的工作環境、不喜歡的工作或上司而考慮辭職。「辭職」的英文是 resign，但是「考慮辭職」不是 *consider to resign。

為甚麼不是 *consider to resign 呢？因為「考慮或想做某事」，後面可以跟兩種結構：動名詞或連接副詞（或連接代詞）＋動詞不定式 to，所以「考慮辭職」的正確英文是 consider resigning / consider going to resign 或 consider whether to resign。其他錯誤例子還有：

他考慮親自去見他們。

✘ He <u>considered</u> to see them in person.

她考慮去日本。

✘ She <u>considered</u> to go to Japan.

那足球員正在考慮移居加拿大。

✘ The football player <u>is considering</u> to emigrate to Canada.

他正在考慮買一輛新車。

✘ He <u>is considering</u> to buy a new car.

上述各句應改為：

他考慮親自見他們。

✔ He <u>considered</u> going to see them in person.

她考慮去日本。

✔ She <u>considered</u> going to Japan.

那足球員正在考慮移居加拿大。

✔ The football player <u>is considering</u> emigrating to Canada.

他正在考慮買一輛新車。

✔ He <u>is considering</u> buying a new car.

另外，留意 consider 等於 think about，所以不需要在 <u>consider</u> 後面用介詞 about。例如：

你應該考慮他的提議。

不是 ✘ You should <u>consider</u> about his suggestion.

而是 ✔ You should <u>consider</u> his suggestion.

2*11* contact 何時與 with 一起用？

日常生活裏經常説「聯絡、聯繫」，英語是 <u>contact</u>。它是名詞，例如：

我和叔叔經常聯絡。

✔ I have much <u>contact</u> with my uncle.

你和你大學裏的朋友還保持聯繫嗎？

✔ Have you kept in <u>contact</u> with any of your friends from the university?

他和女兒失去了聯絡。

✔ He has lost <u>contact</u> with her daughter.

她最終在東京與他取得了聯繫。

✔ She finally made <u>contact</u> with him in Tokyo.

它也是「接觸」的意思。例如：

這種物質不應與食物接觸。

✔ This substance should not come into <u>contact</u> with food.

一瞬間，她的手和我的手碰在一起。

✔ For a moment, her hand was in <u>contact</u> with mine.

注意：contact 也是動詞。但以下是錯誤例子：

如果你有任何問題，儘管和我聯繫。

✘ Please do not hesitate to <u>contact</u> with me if you have any questions.

更詳細的情況請與資訊中心聯繫。

✘ <u>Contact</u> with the Information Centre for further details.

我試着給她的辦公室打電話，但是她不在。

✘ I tried to <u>contact</u> with her at her office, but she wasn't in.

以上三句的錯誤就是在動詞 contact 後面加了 with。正確例子如下：

✔ Please do not hesitate to <u>contact</u> me if you have any questions.

✔ <u>Contact</u> the Information Centre for further details.

✔ I tried to <u>contact</u> her at her office, but she wasn't in.

還有其他正確例子：

✔ Have you contacted her?

✔ Have you made a contact with her?

2.12 demand 甚麼時候後跟 for

在日常生活以至各種正式或非正式會議裏，參加會議的人都會提出各類要求，經常用到 demand 及 request，但使用不正確的例子不少，例如：

他要求道歉。

✗ He demanded for an apology.

他們要求加薪 5%。

✗ They are demanding for a 5% pay rise.

欲知道更多資料，請撥打我們的熱線。

✗ To request for more information, please call our hotline.

拍照必須獲得批准。

✗ You must request for permission if you want to take any photographs.

上述各例子都有錯誤。原來這幾句都不需要介詞 for 的。

但可能大家一定說 demand 和 request 的後面是應該用 for 的。

沒錯！當 demand 和 request 是名詞的時候，它們是需要用介詞 for 的。例如：

其中一個問題是日益增長的住屋需求。

One of the problems is the growing <u>demand</u> for housing.

商業軟件的需求量巨大。

There is a huge <u>demand</u> for business software.

他們緊急要求國際援助。

They have made an urgent <u>request</u> for international aid.

她拒絕了他們會面的要求。

She rejected their <u>request</u> for a meeting.

總之，我們要注意：

當 <u>demand</u> 和 <u>request</u> 是動詞的時候，它們後面是不需要介詞 for 的。

我們不應該把它們跟 ask for 混淆。例如：

請儘管向我要求更多詳細資料。

Please do not hesitate to ask me for more details.

2/3 investigate 用作動詞時不後跟 into

日常生活裏經常說調查或作出調查,但很多時都會用錯。錯誤
例子如下:

警方來調查一宗謀殺案。

✘ The police had come to <u>investigate</u> into a murder.

他們着手調查該社區的民情。

✘ They set out to <u>investigate</u> into the mood of the
community.

她對各種指責作了詳細調查。

✘ She carefully <u>investigated</u> into the allegations.

他應該對謠言作出調查。

✘ He should <u>investigate</u> into the rumour.

第一種錯誤就是在使用動詞 investigate 時,經常把 into 放在後
面。因此,在上述例子,刪去 into 就正確。即是:

✔ The police had come to <u>investigate</u> a murder.

✔ They set out to <u>investigate</u> the mood of the community.

✔ She carefully <u>investigated</u> the allegations.

✔ He should <u>investigate</u> the rumour.

另一種錯誤就是使用名詞 investigation 時,忘記把 into 放在後
面或用錯其他介詞。

正確例子如下：

他們正在對這事進行調查。

They were conducting an <u>investigation</u> into the affair.

對這次意外的調查已經完成。

<u>Investigations</u> into the accident have been completed.

他們並無對該業務進行獨立調查。

They have not conducted any independent <u>investigation</u> into the business.

應建立特別的機制對個案展開調查。

A special mechanism should be established to carry out an <u>investigation</u> into the case.

2.14 表示「放下」、「降低」，low 和 down 不可連用

某大型屋苑的接駁巴士張貼一個告示，上面寫着 *Please <u>low</u> down the volume. ，這句含兩個錯誤，首先， <u>low</u> 是形容詞、副詞和名詞，是「低」的意思，例如：

她跳過了那堵低欄。

She jumped over the <u>low</u> fence.

聲音放低一點。

Keep your voices <u>low</u>.

低薪工人

<u>Low</u>-paid workers

昨晚氣溫降低至有記錄以來的最低點。

The temperature reached a record <u>low</u> last night.

它也是動詞，是發出母牛的叫聲，等於 MOO。

但我們說「放下」不是 <u>low</u> down。

應說 <u>lower</u>，它是動詞。例如：

他們已經降低價錢。

They have <u>lowered</u> the price.

他放下書本周圍看了看。

He <u>lowered</u> his book and looked around.

! NOTES 注意 !

另外，請記着用 <u>lower</u> 解作「放下」時，無需在後面加上 down，因為 <u>lower</u> 已是「放下」的意思，所以 <u>lower</u> down 是錯的。

其他例子還有：

這種藥用來降低血壓。

This drug is used to <u>lower</u> blood pressure.

所以「請小聲點、安靜點」應是 Please <u>lower</u> your voices. 其實說 Keep your voices down. 最好。至於提高或調高電視機或收音機的音量是 <u>increase</u> 或 <u>turn up</u> volume，而「降低或調低音量」是 <u>decrease</u> 或 <u>turn down</u> volume。

215 注意 the morning 之前用 on 或 in 含義不同

對於英語介詞的運用，不少人經常覺得困難，除了因為需要牢記外，主要是使用某些介詞時容易產生混淆。以 <u>on</u> 為例，以下是常見錯誤：

意外在星期日早上 / 晚上發生。

　　不是✘ The accident happened in Sunday morning / night.

　　而是✔ The accident happened <u>on</u> Sunday morning / night.

她聖誕節早上 7 時起牀。

　　不是✘ She got up at 7 o'clock in Christmas morning.

　　而是✔ She got up at 7 o'clock <u>on</u> Christmas morning.

很多人在晴朗的早晨游泳。

　　不是✘ Many people go to the beach in a sunny morning.

　　而是✔ Many people go to the beach <u>on</u> a sunny morning.

產生上述錯誤的原因，主要是因為我們對 in the morning 很熟悉，就以為其他所有 morning 都是使用 in。但在英語，我們說「星期日早上 / 晚上、聖誕節早上、晴朗的早晨」時，英語着重「星期日、聖誕節及晴朗」的一天，所以應該用 <u>on</u>。類似例子還有：

他在復活節晚上去了日本。

　　不是 ✘ He went to Japan in Easter night.

而是 ✔ He went to Japan <u>on</u> Easter night.

我們將會在某日（例如七月十日）的早上 / 下午 / 晚上開會。

    不是 ✘ We will hold a meeting in the morning / afternoon / night of (date, e.g. 10th July).

    而是 ✔ We will hold a meeting <u>on</u> the morning / afternoon / night of (date, e.g. 10th July).

此外，以下例子都是錯誤的：

上星期日食水供應暫停。

    ✘ Water supply was suspended on last Saturday.

工程將會在這星期五開始。

    ✘ The works will commence on this Friday.

下星期一見。

    ✘ See you on next Monday.

他們逢星期一開會。

    ✘ They meet on every Tuesday.

! NOTES 注意 *!*

請大家記着，在 last / this / that / next / every Saturday, etc（上 / 這 / 那 / 下 / 逢星期六）等例子，以至 all day / one day，我們都不應該在它們前面加上 <u>on</u> 的。

2.16 「加上」不是 add up，別隨便用介詞

由於英語介詞 (prepositions) 太多太複雜，很難學得好又容易用錯，所以是常見的英語錯誤。同時，它也是中式英語錯誤的其中一種，因為我們在使用介詞時，很多時候都會因為中文思維而犯錯。以下是一些常見例子：

那學生舉高手。

> 不是 ✘ The student raised up his hand.
>
> 而是 ✔ The student raised his hand.

然後他把手放下。

> 不是 ✘ Then he lowered his hand down.
>
> 而是 ✔ Then he lowered his hand.

她七時返回家裏。

> 不是 ✘ She returned back home at 11 p.m.
>
> 而是 ✔ She returned home at 11 p.m.

大衛將會跟露絲結婚。

> 不是 ✘ David is going to marry with Lucy.
>
> 而是 ✔ David is going to marry Lucy.

他們將會記下你的供詞。

> 不是 ✘ They will record down your statement.
>
> 而是 ✔ They will record your statement.

她想提出問題。

不是 ✘ She wants to raise up a question.

而是 ✔ She wants to raise a question.

記得列出主要問題。

不是 ✘ Remember to list out the major problems.

而是 ✔ Remember to list the major problems.

請降低價錢／聲浪。

不是 ✘ Please lower down the price / voice.

而是 ✔ Please lower the price / voice.

從上述例子可以看到那些句裏的介詞是中文直譯，但原句的動詞其實不需要那些介詞。即是説「舉高」是 raise，不需加 up、所以「舉高手」是 raise your hand，「放下」是 lower，不需加 down、「返回」是 return，不需加 back、「跟別人結婚」是 marry，不需加 with、「記下」是 record、不需加 down「提出」是 raise，不需加 up、「列出」是 list，不需加 out、「降低」是 lower，不需加 down、「加上」是 add，不需加上 up。add up 是「説得通、似乎有道理」的意思。上述幾個動詞後面全部不需要介詞。當然有人可能説加上相關介詞後，大家仍會明白句子的意思，不過那不是正確的英語。只要大家小心就能避免犯錯。

2.17 別在 start 、 begin 和 commence 之後錯用 from

由於我們經常説「開始」，所以英文 start 、 begin 和 commence 也在日常公文裏出現，但很可惜，不少人説「從時間 / 數目開始」時，都會説 start 、 begin 或 commence from ，但那是錯誤的。錯誤例子如下：

會議從 9 時開始。

✘ The meeting <u>starts / commences</u> from 9.

修築新路的工程將在下月開始。

✘ Work on the new road will <u>begin</u> from next month.

比賽從 9 時開始。

✘ The game <u>starts</u> from 9.

她每天早上 8:30 開始工作。

✘ She <u>started</u> work from 8:30 every morning.

房子的號碼從 10 開始。

✘ The house numbers <u>start</u> from 10.

他在晨曦 / 中午開始上路。

✘ He <u>started</u> his journey from dawn / noon.

上述各個例子裏都不應該用 from，而應該改說 at 9 / 8:30 / 10 / dawn，因為會議 / 比賽在 9 時那一刻開始，她的工作在 8:30 那一刻開始，而房子號碼及上路開始的英文也應該用 at。而「工程將在下月開始」，就不需要用介詞。我們用了 from，主要是由於中文是「從」，由於我們受到中文的「從」影響，因此我們不知道那是錯的。

事實上，我們要明白，start、begin 及 commence 一些事情，是說從某一時間點開始工作或行動。例如：

父親十七歲開始工作。

My father <u>started</u> work when he was seventeen.

他們計劃今天開始絕食。

They plan to <u>begin</u> a hunger strike today.

他開始一輪探訪。

He <u>commenced</u> a round of visits.

但我們說時間或數目的開始，必須說得準確。例如：

一系列的新體育節目已開始在星期一播出。

A new series of sports programme <u>has started</u> on Monday.

你可以星期一就來上班嗎？

Can you <u>start</u> (a new job) on Monday?

因為新體育節目在星期一播出，你在星期一上班，說 from

Monday 就不對，改為 on Monday 才準確。

酒店的雙人房間一晚一千元起。

Hotel prices <u>start</u> at $1,000 a night for a double room.

如果大家仍然不明白，嘗試改說結束 end / finish 就會明白。因為在一個準確的時間結束，所以沒理由用 from。例如：

會議星期五結束。

The conference ends on Friday.

比賽在 10 時結束了。

The game finished at 10 o'clock.

3

用詞混淆

31 「虛幻」、「想像」、「臆測」用 imaginary 還是 imaginative？

我們經常說「幻想」、「虛幻」、「臆測」、「虛構」、「虛無縹緲」和「富想像力」、「充滿想像力」，英語是 <u>imaginary</u> 和 <u>imaginative</u>，但很多時候會令人混淆，造成錯誤。以下是錯誤的例子：

富想像力的人

   ✘ an <u>imaginary</u> man

虛構的人

   ✘ an <u>imaginative</u> man

充滿想像的設計

   ✘ <u>imaginary</u> design

虛幻的景象

   ✘ <u>imaginative</u> images

我們需要對設計富想像力。

   ✘ We need to be <u>imaginary</u> about the design.

他們不會應對幻想的恐懼。

   ✘ They will not entertain <u>imaginative</u> fears.

導致以上錯誤的原因是我們混淆了 <u>imaginary</u> 和 <u>imaginative</u>。

其實 imaginary 是「幻想」、「虛幻」、「臆測」、「虛構」或「虛無縹緲」的意思，而 imaginative 是「富想像力」或「充滿想像力」的意思。

其他正確例子還有：

他們所支持的都是虛無縹緲。

✔ What they are supporting is purely imaginary.

他們的憂慮大多出於幻想。

✔ Most of their worries were only imaginary.

這本書裏所有人物都是虛構的。

✔ All the characters in this book are imaginary.

這位年青作家富於想像力。

✔ The young writer is quite imaginative.

這些挑戰需要充滿想像力的對策。

✔ The challenges required imaginative responses.

主考人希望有創見的答案。

✔ The examiners are looking for imaginative answers.

32 instead 須後接 something 或 doing something

instead 是「代替、改為、而不是」的意思。例如：

天氣太熱，不適宜散步，我們改為游泳吧。

It's too hot to go for a walk; let's go swimming <u>instead</u>.

如果她不想去，我就替你去好了。

If she doesn't want to go, I'll go <u>instead</u>.

那項目應改為在七月一日開始。

The project should commence on 1 July <u>instead</u>.

但以下例子是錯誤的：

他應該在工作而不該在牀上睡覺。

✘ He should be working <u>instead</u> to sleep in bed.

你會代替經理去開會嗎？

✘ Will you go to the meeting <u>instead</u> to the manager?

她沒有吃披薩，只吃了沙律。

✘ She just had salad <u>instead</u> to pizza.

他們選中她，沒選我。

✘ They chose her <u>instead</u> to me.

現在你可以步行上學，而不是乘坐巴士了。

✘ Now you can walk to school <u>instead</u> to go by bus.

在上述例子，<u>instead</u> 後面應該用 of 而不是 to。

其他正確例子還有：

她買了一輛舊車，不是新的。

<u>Instead</u> of buying a new car, she bought a used one.

他在七點鐘而不是六點鐘吃飯。

He had his meal at seven o'clock <u>instead</u> of six o'clock.

他們喝咖啡代替牛奶。

They had coffee <u>instead</u> of milk.

她循環再用那些廢紙，沒有扔掉它。

<u>Instead</u> of throwing away the scrap paper, she recycled it.

33 manage 可以和 can 一起用嗎？

<u>manage</u> 解作 "成功做到" 或 "順利完成"。<u>manage</u> 後跟帶 to 的動詞。例如：

在購物商場迷了路的小孩最終順利找回自己的媽媽。

> ✔ The child who got lost in the shopping mall finally <u>managed</u> to find his mother.

馬克告訴我你有可能把我的平板電腦修理好。

> ✔ Mark told me that you might <u>manage</u> to repair my tablet.

但當 manage 的意思是 "能做到" 時，就不可在它前面加 can 或 could。

以下是錯誤例子：

我弟弟沒有通過期終考試。

> ✘ My little brother could not <u>manage</u> to pass the final exam.

我無法修理好你的平板電腦。

> ✘ I could not manage to repair your tablet.

上述例子應改為：

> ✔ My little brother did not <u>manage</u> to pass the final exam.
> ✔ I did not <u>manage</u> to repair your tablet.

此外，<u>manage</u> 有"管理"的意思。以下是錯誤例子：

他安排書在下月寄送到客戶手上。

✘ He will manage that books are sent to the client next month.

上述例子應改為：

✔ He will arrange for the books to be sent to the client next month.

! NOTES 注意 !

不要混淆 <u>manage</u> 和 arrange。arrange 是"安排"、"籌備"的意思。<u>manage</u> 是"管理"某項目或業務的意思。

3.4 「麻煩事」、「毛病」、「失常」，到底該用 matter 還是 problem 呢？

我們經常説 <u>matter</u>，它是「事情、問題」的意思。至於 the <u>matter</u> 就是「麻煩事、困難」的意思。例如 What's the <u>matter</u>?; Why are you crying? 是「怎麼回事？你為甚麼哭？」There's nothing the <u>matter</u>. 或 Nothing is the <u>matter</u> with him. 是「沒事，他沒有甚麼。」的意思。 What's the <u>matter</u> with the television? Why isn't it working? 是「電視機出了甚麼問題啦？怎麼不能看了？」The <u>matter</u> with us is that we haven't enough time. 就是「我們的問題是時間不夠。」

近年不少人在上述例子用了 problem 代替 <u>matter</u>，但那是不對的。為甚麼呢？

那是因為 <u>matter</u> 是「普通的事情、問題」的意思，而 the <u>matter</u> 用作「麻煩事、困難」時，是指「不正常、失常」的情況。簡單來説，那「麻煩事、困難」是「毛病」的意思。因此，There is nothing the <u>matter</u> with the machine. 是説「這機器沒有毛病。」

現在來看看 problem。它是 a difficulty that needs attention and thought 即「難題、困難」。例如：

我們面對的難題是資金缺乏。

　　✔ The problem we face is the lack of fund.

困難在於我們需要主席的最後批准，但主席正在放假。

　　✔ The problem is that we need the Chairman's final

approval, but the Chairman is on leave.

那政策將會解決失業難題。

　✔ The policy can solve the problem of unemployment.

他們將會討論繁忙時間交通擠塞的問題。

　✔ They will discuss the problem of traffic congestion during peak hours.

從上述各句可看到 problem 與 <u>matter</u> 的區別，最重要的是 problem 是「需要解決的問題」，不是「不正常、失常」的情況、「麻煩事、困難」的意思。因此以上各句不可用 <u>matter</u> 代替。

另一方面，have a problem with something 有特別的意思，它指 to disagree with or object to something 即「對……有異議；不同意；反對」。例如：

你在家工作，我沒有意見。

　✔ I have no problem with you working at home.

在非正式的用法裏，Do you have a problem with that? 是「你有甚麼意見嗎？」的意思。

所以 no problem 或 not a problem 就是「沒問題」。

至於 What's your problem? 是「你怎麼了？」。

3.5 「記住」、「記得」、「記起」用 memorise 還是 remember？

很多人不能區分 memorise 與 remember，因而出現以上錯誤。remember 只是記起的意思，而記在心裏是 memorise。

以下例子看來沒錯，但其實都是錯誤的：

他記住演講詞。

不是 ✘ He remembered the speech.

而是 ✔ He memorised the speech.

我記下所有條款。

不是 ✘ I shall remember all the terms and conditions.

而是 ✔ I shall memorise all the terms and conditions.

她深深記住了他。

不是 ✘ She memorised him very well.

而是 ✔ She remembered him very well.

其實，memorise 是 to learn something carefully so that you can remember it exactly。它就是「熟記、背誦」的意思。

請看看以下兩句的區別：

They memorised the lesson. 是 "他們記住這課堂。" 的意思，只是 "一時的動作"，而 They remembered the lesson. 是 "他們記

得這課堂。"的意思，並不是"一時的動作"。

其他正確例子還有：

我會嘗試記住詳情。

✔ I shall try to <u>memorise</u> the details.

他能夠在 3 分鐘內記住一首詩的內容。

✔ He was able to <u>memorise</u> a poem within three minutes.

我會嘗試記起他的面孔。

✔ I shall try to remember his face.

我會嘗試記起她的房子。

✔ I shall try to remember her house.

36 no sooner... than 在句首時，主語和動詞須換位

no sooner... than 的句式很常用，但我們使用時必須注意三點：

1. no sooner 後面通常使用過去完成時態 (past perfect tense)；
2. 在句首時，主語要和動詞或助動詞換位。
3. no sooner 與 than 連用而不是 when。

以下是錯誤例子：

預算案剛剛公佈戰爭就在中東爆發。

> 不是 ✘ No sooner the budget was announced than war broke out in the Middle East.

> 而是 ✔ No sooner had the budget been announced than war broke out in the Middle East.

政策剛剛推出他們就想到對策了。

> 不是 ✘ No sooner the policy was implemented than they thought up counter-measures.

> 而是 ✔ No sooner had the policy been implemented than they thought up counter-measures.

我剛拿起報紙電話就響起了。

> 不是 ✘ No sooner I took up the newspaper than the telephone rang.

> 而是 ✔ No sooner had I taken up the newspaper than the

telephone rang.

我一敲門他就開門了。

不是 ✘ No sooner I knocked than he opened the door.

而是 ✔ <u>No sooner</u> had I knocked <u>than</u> he opened the door.

我們剛到達目的地就下雨了。

不是 ✘ No sooner had we reached the destination when it began to rain.

而是 ✔ No sooner had we reached the destination <u>than</u> it began to rain.

其他正確例子還有：

我們剛剛坐下就發現該走了。

<u>No sooner</u> had we sat down <u>than</u> we found it was time to go.

他剛剛上任就暗示職能將會重組。

<u>No sooner</u> had he taken office <u>than</u> he hinted that the functions would be reorganized.

她剛說完就哭起來了。

<u>No sooner</u> had she said it <u>than</u> she burst into tears.

他剛合上眼就睡着了。

<u>No sooner</u> had he closed his eyes <u>than</u> he fell asleep.

! NOTES 注意 *!*

No sooner said than done 是「說到做到、立刻」的意思，與上述句式無關。例如：Can you close the door? No sooner said than done. 是「關上門好嗎？立刻就做。」的意思。

3.7　oblige 用 SVO 還是 it 句式

oblige 是「必須、不得不、有義務 / 責任」的意思，但它的句式不是 It oblige somebody to do something。以下是錯誤例子：

我必須與他們共用房子。

不是 ✘ It obliged me to share the house with them.

而是 ✔ I felt obliged to share the house with them.

他必須尋找工作。

不是 ✘ It obliged him to find a job.

而是 ✔ He is obliged to find a job.

她不得不邀請他們吃飯。

不是 ✘ It obliged her to ask them to dinner.

而是 ✔ She felt obliged to ask them to dinner.

父母不得不送子女讀書。

不是 ✘ It obliged parents to send their children to school.

而是 ✔ Parents are obliged to send their children to school.

政府必須向市民公開該文件。

不是 ✘ It obliged the government to release the document to the public.

而是 ✔ The government is obliged to release the document to the public.

其他正確例子還有：

他們無須向他發出選舉權的通知。

✔ They shall not be <u>obliged</u> to give to him notice of the right of election.

他不得不停止所有活動。

✔ He is <u>obliged</u> to freeze all activity.

僱員有義務在合同指定的時間工作。

✔ The employee is <u>obliged</u> to work in the hours specified in the contract.

她認為有責任了解情況。

✔ She felt <u>obliged</u> to understand the situation.

他們不得不對決議草案投反對票。

✔ They felt <u>obliged</u> to vote against the draft resolution.

! NOTES 注意 !

I am much <u>obliged</u> (to somebody) (for something / for doing something) 是正式用語，它是「感激、感謝」的意思。例如：I am much <u>obliged</u> to you for helping us. ，意思是「承蒙相助，本人不勝感激」。

38 unique 可以與 so、rather 等一起用嗎？

我們説一個人或事物「獨一無二、唯一、獨特」的時候，都會像中文加上程度修飾語如「很、更加、最」，即 so、very、rather、more、most 等，但這是不對的。以下是錯誤例子：

獨一無二的機會

✘ very <u>unique</u> opportunity

獨有特色

✘ so <u>unique</u> feature

唯一特徵

✘ very <u>unique</u> characteristic

每個人的指紋是獨一無二的。

✘ Everyone's fingerprints are most <u>unique</u>.

樹熊是澳洲獨有的。

✘ The Koala is so <u>unique</u> to Australia.

她的才能使她獨一無二。

✘ Her talents make her very <u>unqiue</u>.

總之，我們要記着 <u>unique</u> 用作「獨一無二、唯一、獨特」的意思時，不可加 so、very、rather、more、most，只可用

almost 、 absolutely 或 totally 修飾。

almost <u>unique</u> 就是「堪稱無可匹敵」。 absolutely / totally <u>unique</u> 就是「絕對、完全獨一無二」。

其他常用例子還有：

網域內的使用者會收到他自己的獨有帳戶。

Users within the domain receive his own <u>unique</u> account.

聯合國的建議考慮到每個國家的獨特情況。

UN's advice takes into account the <u>unique</u> situation of each country.

我們希望共同為未來領袖創建一個獨有平台。

Together we hope to build a <u>unique</u> platform for future leaders.

3.9 「景色」、「景象」到底用 sight 還是 view？

英文 view 和 sight 都是看到的景象的意思，但兩者有些不同。view 通常指遠處的景象。即從特定處所看到的景色、視域、視野、視力。例如：

為了更好地看一看海港，他上了大廈天台。

✔ To get a better view of the harbour, he went to the roof of the building.

我們登上山頂，遼闊的平原盡收眼底。

✔ When we reached the top of the mountain, a wide plain came into view.

請給他一間窗外景色不錯的房間。

✔ He would like a room with a good view.

她看不清舞台。

✔ She did not have a good view of the stage.

簡單來說，view 是指從某處看到的景色、風光，尤指自然美景。

另一方面，sight 是指看見或看得見的事物、景象，尤指壯觀、奇特的景象。例子：

她朝街上望去，一個人也沒看見。

✔ She looked up the street, but there was no one in sight.

我在海上航行十天之後，首次看見陸地。

✔ After ten days at sea, I had my first sight of land.

大家都知道，她看到血就會昏倒。

✔ She has been known to faint at the sight of blood.

最後眼前出現了一輛公共汽車。

✔ At last, a bus came into sight.

你應該時常留意你的手袋。

✔ You should always keep sight of your handbag.

! NOTES 注意 *!*

caught sight of = saw for a moment，即看到了。
lost sight of = could no longer see，即看不見了。

3.10 voice 可以和 speak with 一起用嗎？

日常生活裏經常說「用……聲音說話」，例如「很高 / 大 / 低 / 輕柔 / 低沉 / 膽怯 / 輕的聲音」，英語是 a loud / high / low / soft / deep / timid / quiet <u>voice</u>，但在完整句子配合 speak / talk / say 使用時，我們該用 in 而不是 with。以下是正確例子：

她低 / 小聲說。

    ✔ She said in a low / small voice. = 輕聲 / 害羞的聲音 quiet / shy <u>voice</u>

他輕聲說話。

    ✔ He spoke in a quiet <u>voice</u>.

她大聲說話。

    ✔ She spoke in a very loud <u>voice</u>.

雖然他們大聲說話，畢竟無勇氣講出心底訴求。

    ✔ Although they speak in a loud <u>voice</u>, they have no courage to say what they are thinking in their inmost heart.

嘶啞 / 沙啞 / 粗魯的嗓音

    A hoarse / husky / rough <u>voice</u>

注意：with one <u>voice</u> 與上述例子不同，它是「指很多人齊聲、一致或異口同聲地說話」。它是正式用語，例如：

該議會感到在這件事上，他們必須立場一致。

✔ The Council felt that they should speak on the matter with one voice.

該委員會作出決議，一致同意接受那項建議。

✔ The Committee decided with one voice to accept the proposal.

另外，at the top of one's voice 是「扯着喉嚨、放開嗓子、喊、唱」的意思。我們不該用 with 或 in。例如：

他大聲疾呼虐兒不可容忍。

✔ He is shouting at the top of his voice that child abuse should not be tolerated.

3.11 十億和一億有天淵之別，別混淆
billion 和 million

曾經有一次六合彩的估計頭獎彩金可以高達一億元，當年在某個投注站裏，它的「多寶」告示寫着 Estimated First Division Fund: $1 <u>BILLION</u> ，但 $1 <u>BILLION</u> 不是「一億元」，這是非常嚴重的錯誤，因為 $1 billion 是十億元，不是一億元，而是一億元的十倍。

很多同學和在職人士都弄不清楚 billion，但從今天起請大家記着 1 billion 不是一億，而是十億。中文一億是 one hundred million。

其實，我們看看英文就明白。首先，在數學上：

一串數字最後有 3 個 0 是 thousand。例子：1 thousand 是 1,000；

一串數字最後有 6 個 0 是 million。例子：1 million 是 1,000,000。

而 1 <u>billion</u> 指 1 後面有 9 個 0 即 1,000,000,000 即「十億」。

大家如果仍然記不住，可以用中國人常用的計算方法數一數。即是從右邊結尾開始向左數：就會是「個、十、百、千、萬、十萬、百萬、千萬、億、十億」。圖示如下：

1,000,000,000

十億 億 千萬 百萬 十萬 萬 千 百 十 個

所以 1,000,000,000 是「十億」。

大家可能問中文數目的「個、十、百、千、萬、十萬、百萬、千萬」之後不是萬萬嗎？那當然「萬萬不可」！記着「千萬」之後是「億」。例如：

中國人口有十四億。

   ✔ China has a population of 1.4 billion.

絕對不是 14 billion。

14 billion 是「一百四十億」。

其他例子還有：

去年世界銷量達 35 億。

   ✔ Worldwide sales reached 3.5 billion last year.

我們已經花費數十億元來解決這問題。

   ✔ We have spent billions of dollars on the problem.

3.12 condition 可數或不可數必須分清楚

condition 是常用詞，但使用時要注意單數和複數的區別。condition 不能用來指一個具體的情況，而用來指某人或物所處的情況／狀況／狀態時必須是單數，即 in bad／good／excellent／perfect condition。例如：

這病人情況危急。

> ✓ The patient is in a critical condition.

這大廈狀況良好。

> ✓ The building was still in a good condition.

那些書桌情況良好。

> ✓ The desks are in good condition.

那輛舊車性能一流。

> ✓ The used car is in perfect condition.

複數的 conditions 指某人或物身處的外在環境或情況。例如：

他們的居住環境不佳。

> ✓ Their living conditions are bad.

他居住在擠迫的環境。

✔ He lives in crowded <u>conditions</u>.

經濟狀況不斷變化。

✔ The economic <u>conditions</u> are changing.

這些樹木最適宜在陰涼潮濕的環境下生長。

✔ The trees grow best in cool, damp <u>conditions</u>.

簡單來說 condition 指內在情況而 conditions 指外在環境。

所以上文的「工作情況不理想」應改為 The working <u>conditions</u> are not satisfactory. 。

至於用作「條件、條款」意思的 <u>condition</u> 是可數名詞，單數或複數也可以。例如：

僱傭條款

✔ Terms and conditions of employment.

第二項條件主要是避免不公平

✔ The second condition is intended to avoid unfairness.

3.13 禮多人不怪，別忘記加 s

congratulations 是常用詞，它是「祝賀、恭喜」的意思。但很多時我們會忘記它一般是複數。同學經常問為甚麼？我笑說我們恭喜別人時，不是會說多過一次的恭喜嗎？「恭喜！恭喜！」在英文裏，有些抽象名詞會以複數形式來表示強調，例如 thanks、wishes、apologies 及 kindnesses 等。例如：

謝謝你借錢給我。

✔ Thanks for lending me money.

我們都對未來致以最好的祝願。

✔ We all send our best wishes for the future.

他致歉後就提前離開了。

✔ He made his apologies and left early.

我無法報答你對我無微不至的關懷。

✔ I can never repay your many kindnesses to me.

congratulations 的其他例子：

向所有獲勝者祝賀！

✔ Congratulations to all the winners!

恭喜你結婚！

✔ Congratulations on your marriage!

見到她務必請代我向她祝賀。

✔ Please give her / pass on my <u>congratulations</u> when you see her.

我們向他致以最衷心的祝賀。

✔ We offer him the heartiest <u>congratulations</u>.

! NOTES 注意 *!*

「祝賀信」A note of <u>congratulation</u>, a letter of <u>congratulation</u> 可用單數。例如：

她選舉獲勝，我們寄出祝賀信。

✔ We sent her a note of <u>congratulation</u> on her election victory.

3.14 criticise 可與 that 子句一起用嗎？

日常生活裏經常説「批評」，它的英語是 <u>criticism</u> 或 <u>criticise</u>。criticism 是名詞，它比較簡單，可以用 that 加子句。但它的動詞 <u>criticise</u> 的運用就不同。記着：我們批評 <u>criticise</u> 某人、某事或 for doing 某事，而不用 that 加子句。以下是錯誤例子：

她批評這是錯誤的決定。

✘ She <u>criticised</u> that the decision was wrong.

他批評該部門沒有認真處理這問題。

✘ He <u>criticised</u> that the department had not taken the problem seriously.

他們因該案處理得不好而受到批評。

✘ They were <u>criticized</u> that the case was handled badly.

公司被批評對員工醫療福利的投資不夠。

✘ The company was <u>criticised</u> that investment in employee health benefits was not enough.

以上各句應改為：

✔ She <u>criticised</u> the wrong decision.

✔ He <u>criticised</u> the department for not taking the problem seriously.

✔ They were <u>criticised</u> for handling the case badly.

✔ The company was <u>criticised</u> for failing to invest enough in employee health benefits.

其他正確例子還有：

那條法律受到批評，指其牽涉種族主義問題。

   ✔ The law was <u>criticised</u> as racist.

他總是批評他的妻子馬虎。

   ✔ He <u>has</u> always <u>been criticising</u> his wife for being sloppy.

他們批評電視有害。

   ✘ They <u>criticised</u> TV is harmful.

應說

   ✔ They <u>criticised</u> TV as being harmful. 或

   ✔ They <u>criticised</u> TV, saying that it is harmful.

或不用 <u>criticised</u>，改為

   ✔ They said that TV is harmful.

3.15 「橫跨」用 cross 還是 across ?

我曾在某醫院行人過路處看到告示出現英文錯誤，就馬上告訴那醫院的行政部門，說 *across the road 不對，應該是 <u>cross</u> the road。不久，那告示果然不見了。到了新告示出現，卻只有中文版，沒有了英文版。想不到竟然因為害怕再犯錯而不寫英文。如果我們學習英語時都抱着這種態度，那就沒有進步的機會了。

從上述例子可以看到發出告示的人把「過馬路」誤寫成 *across the road，可能是由於以為 across 是動詞，所以放在 the road 前面，也可能是混淆了動詞 cross 而寫錯。例如：

他們用了兩天時間越過沙漠。

　　✔ They took two days to <u>cross</u> the desert.

你要看清楚沒有車輛才過馬路。

　　✔ Make sure that there is no traffic before you <u>cross</u> the road.

另一個出錯的原因可能是不知道 across 是副詞和介詞，它是必須配合相關動詞運用的。例如：

他在河上建了一座橋。

　　✔ He built a bridge across the river.

她就住在馬路的對面。

　　✔ She lives just across the road.

我扶這位老先生過馬路。

> ✔ I helped the old man across the road. (= I helped him to cross it.)

其實，上述例子也說明了學會英文語法的重要性。

如果我們知道英文句子的基本結構是主語 (subject) 和動詞 (verb)，即 S + V；或 主語 (subject)、動詞 (verb) 和 賓語 (object) 即 S + V + O，就不會誤寫成 *Please across the road 了。

希望大家學好語法規則。

當然，有人會問怎樣才知道 cross 是動詞，across 是副詞和介詞呀？那自然是查閱英語詞典了。

3.16 「杯」不一定是 cup

相信大家對 cup 這個英文非常熟悉，連幼稚園學生都知道它是「杯子」的意思。例如茶杯 (teacup)、咖啡杯 (coffee cup)、紙杯 (paper cup)、蛋杯 (egg cup)、杯碟 (a cup and saucer) 以至各類公開比賽的獎盃。近年不少人喜愛的 cupcake 就是紙杯蛋糕，而這些杯子通常是有杯耳的。

這裏我想起多年前一個小故事，它是在一家連鎖快餐店發生的。當時有個外籍女傭到櫃台向服務員說 Please give me a <u>cup</u>.，那個年青男服務員說聲 ok，然後馬上去拿。但他回來時，手裏拿着一個玻璃杯。那個女傭驚訝一兩秒，然後拿着那個玻璃杯返回她的桌子。

我不知道那女傭是不是真的想要玻璃杯，但她說的是 cup，而那個男服務員拿給她的卻是一個玻璃杯，他可能不明白甚麼是 <u>cup</u>，也可能他以為玻璃杯是 cup，又或者他不懂得 glass 是玻璃杯，以為 <u>cup</u> 是玻璃杯。當然也有可能是他發現當時沒有 <u>cup</u> 而只找到 glass，所以拿了玻璃杯給她。

其實，很多人平日都會說 cup。那就是英語的習慣用語 Not my <u>cup</u> of tea，那是「非我所好、不合我心意」的意思。例如：

她這人挺不錯，但不是我特別喜歡的那種人。

She's nice enough but really not my <u>cup</u> of tea.

謝謝你邀請我，不過我不大喜歡看高爾夫球。

Thanks for inviting me, but golf isn't really my <u>cup</u> of tea.

請留意：大一點又較高身的塑膠、金屬或瓷製的杯子是 mug。

至於 glass，因為它是用玻璃製成的，所以叫做 glass 玻璃杯。
例如：

A beer / wine glass
啤酒 / 葡萄酒杯

! NOTES 注意 *!*

英文是沒有 a beer / wine cup 的。另外，glasses 是「眼鏡」的意思，一定是複數的。

3.17 破壞嚴重不是 damages

我們經常說要學好英語首先要打好語法基礎。其實這個不難，我們要先了解英語的各種詞類 (parts of speech)。

以名詞為例，我們必須明白甚麼是可數名詞 (countable noun) 及不可數名數 (uncountable noun)。簡單來說，我們應該知道句子裏的名詞應是單數還是複數，因為很多時候名詞的單數和複數意思是不同的。颱風造成的損毀 damage 是沒有複數的。例如：

颱風造成許多損毀。

The typhoon caused a lot of <u>damage</u>.

這些化學物質造成了嚴重的環境破壞。

These chemicals have caused serious environmental <u>damage</u>.

這可能有永久腦損傷。

There may be permanent brain <u>damage</u>.

他的視力遭到無可修復的損傷。

His eyesight suffered irreparable <u>damage</u>.

至於 damages 則是「法院就某人遭受的損害、損傷、損毀或苦難所判定的損害賠償」。例如：

他因受傷獲判一百萬元賠償。

He was awarded $1 million <u>damages</u> for his injury.

他要求十萬元的賠償。

He claimed $100,000 in <u>damages</u>.

在一篇文章裏如果有很多單複數的簡單錯誤，那麼屬於其他類型的錯誤也會很多。這除了影響公開試的分數不高之外，也會使讀者懷疑你的語言能力。

例如吃飯前洗手的英文是 Wash your hand 還是 hands 嗎？賊人搶劫時會叫你 Put up your hand 還是 hands 呢？

檢查眼睛或看眼科醫生的時候，你明白 open / close your eye 和 eyes 的不同意思嗎？

其實，英語詞典在名詞後面都會說明某個名詞是可數還是不可數的。u 就是不可數；p, pl. 或 plural 就代表複數。

3.18 小心分辨 discuss 和 discussion 的用法

在公司或機構的會議紀錄裏，如果說到討論，最常見的錯誤是
✘ discuss about。例如：

他們簡短討論該建議。

不是 ✘ They <u>discussed</u> about the proposal briefly.

而是 ✓ They <u>discussed</u> the proposal briefly.

委員會上星期二開會討論這項議題。

不是 ✘ The committee met to <u>discuss</u> about the issue last Tuesday.

而是 ✓ The committee met to <u>discuss</u> the issue last Tuesday.

這是因為 <u>discuss</u> 用作動詞時，後面是不用加介詞 about 的。

出現這個錯誤，主要是因為大家混淆了動詞 discuss 和名詞 discussion 的用法。

只有我們用名詞 <u>discussion</u> 的時候，後面才會加上介詞 about。

所以上述兩句也可以寫成：

> They had a <u>discussion</u> about the proposal.

The committee met to have a <u>discussion</u> about the issue.

其他例子還有：

他們詳細討論了這項計劃。

> They <u>discussed</u> the plan in great detail.

他想稍後才討論這個問題。

> He'd like to <u>discuss</u> the matter later.

她不願意在電話討論這個問題。

> She was not prepared to <u>discuss</u> this on the phone.

他們就政治改革進行了討論。

> They had a <u>discussion</u> about political reform.

就新聞自由的定義爆發了一場激烈討論。

> An intense <u>discussion</u> broke out about the definition of press freedom.

他們討論未來的計劃。

> They <u>discussed</u> future plans. 或 They had a <u>discussion</u> about future plans.

3.19 注意 indirect question 有特定的詞序

我們在日常生活裏經常説「你知道她為甚麼⋯⋯？」的這類「間接問題」。

在上述例子，我們看到：

> **你知道** = Do you know

> **她為甚麼拒絕？** = Why did she object?

這句子看來是對的，但其實它是錯誤的，它不是正確的「間接問題」。例如：

你知道她為甚麼反對？

> 不是 ✘ Do you know why did she object?

> 而是 ✔ Do you know why she objected?

其實，這是因為我們使用「間接疑問句」indirect questions 時，忘記了需要改變「特殊疑問句」詞序。請記着：

a.「特殊疑問句」是指帶有「特殊疑問詞」(如 who、where、why 等詞)、而且不能用 yes 和 no 直接作答的疑問句。

b. 把「特殊疑問句」改為「間接疑問句」時候，必須注意「從句」部份必須套用「陳述句」語序，即「動詞」放在「主語」後面。

即是說從句部份必須是「陳述句」而不是「疑問句」。其他類似例子還有：

他奇怪瑪麗為甚麼缺席。

He wonders <u>why Mary is absent</u>.

我不知道陳先生說甚麼。

I don't know <u>what Mr Chan said</u>.

彼德將告訴我們那男人年紀有多大。

Peter will tell us <u>how old the man is</u>.

大衛不肯定蘇珊住在哪裏。

David is not sure <u>where Susan works</u>.

愛美想知道露絲是不是在派對裏。

Emily wants to know <u>if Lucy is at the party</u>.

我們必須找出王先生是不是快將離開。

We must find out <u>if Mr Wong is going to leave</u>.

3.20 分辨 due to、for this reason、owing to

due to 是常用詞，解作「由於，因為」是 because of、caused by 的意思。例如：

她的成功完全是勤力的結果。

Her success is entirely due to hard work.

他們的利潤增加主要是由於市場策略成功。

Their increase in profits is largely due to their successful market strategy.

由於發生意外，他沒有來。

His absence was due to the accident.

近年出現了以下相當於 owing to 的用法，也視為正確：

由於大雨，她來遲了。

She arrived late due / owing to the heavy rain.

由於王先生遲到，會議過了六時仍然繼續。

Due / owing to Mr Wong's arriving late, the meeting went on past 6 o'clock.

由於缺乏撥款，這項工程不得不暫停。

The project had to be suspended due / owing to a lack of funding.

但注意以下錯誤例子：

這可能由於惡劣的天氣。

不是 ✘ This may <u>due to</u> the bad weather.

而是 ✔ This may be <u>due to</u> the bad weather.

由於這個原因那商店結業了。

不是 ✘ Due to this reason, the shop was closed down.

而是 ✔ For this reason, the shop was closed down.

這是由於香港租金高昂。

不是 ✘ This is <u>due to</u> Hong Kong rents are high.

而是 ✔ This is <u>due to</u> the high rents in Hong Kong.

或改為 This is because Hong Kong rents are high.

或 This is because of the high rents in Hong Kong.

由於天氣太冷，他們去不了海灘。

不是 ✘ <u>Due to</u> the weather was so cold, they could not go to the beach.

而是 ✔ <u>Due to</u> the cold weather, they could not go to the beach.

或改為 Because the weather was so cold, they could not go to the beach.

或 Because of the cold weather, they could not go to the beach.

3.21 移民是 immigrate 還是 emigrate？

近來很多香港人又說移民了。林博士很想移居泰國，Dr. Lam wants to <u>immigrate</u> to Thailand.。姓張的一家正在移居加拿大了 The Cheungs <u>are immigrating</u> to Canada.。這些又是典型的中式英語。為甚麼呢？

這主要是由於 <u>immigrate</u> 是「移入」的意思，而它的名詞是 <u>immigration</u>，即由外地移入的意思。例如：

1958 年露絲和丈夫攜同子女移居香港。

Lucy and her husband <u>immigrated</u> to Hong Kong with their children in 1958.

這十多年以來，不斷有高學歷和高才能的人士移居香港。

Many people with high education qualifications and skills <u>immigrated</u> to Hong Kong over this past decade or so.

但如果我們從香港移居外地，應說 <u>emigrate</u>，它的名詞是 <u>immigration</u>。例如：

他不返回中國大陸，也不前往外國。

He will not go back to the Mainland China, nor will he <u>emigrate</u> to other countries.

他們有移居其他國家的自由。

They have freedom of <u>emigration</u> to other countries.

她想移居較富裕的國家。

She wants to <u>emigrate</u> to wealthier countries.

同時，香港的 Immigration Department 叫入境處，那是因為該部門的工作主要是管制進入香港而不是離開香港的人，所以它的櫃台叫 Immigration Counter。至於香港很多人叫入境處做移民局，那只是一般叫法。入境處的工作與香港人移民無關。

其他例子還有：

她要求實施共同的入境政策。

She called for a common policy on <u>immigration</u>.

他父母在他三歲時移民這裏。

His parents <u>immigrated</u> here when he was three.

他年輕時移居日本。

He <u>emigrated</u> to Japan as a young man.

十九世紀數以百萬計的德國人從歐洲移民到了美國。

Millions of Germans <u>emigrated</u> from Europe to America in the 1900s.

黃先生移居了日本。

Mr. Wong has <u>emigrated</u> to Japan.

3.22 enter 後加 into 是甚麼意思？

enter 是動詞。例如：

罷工正進入第三週。

The strike is entering its third week.

他們進入課室。

They entered the classroom.

子彈是從哪個部位進入身體的？

Where did the bullet enter the body?

法官進入法庭時所有人都起立。

Everybody stands up when the judge enters the court.

! NOTES 注意 !

enter 作「進入、開始」的意思時是不需要加 into 的。

---

enter into 是「簽訂協議、開始做某事」的意思。例如：

她開始解釋。

She entered into explanation.

他與該公司簽訂為期三年的合約。

He <u>entered into</u> a three-year contract with the company.

我們與他們建立夥伴關係。

We <u>entered into</u> a partnership with them.

<u>entry</u> 是「進入」的意思，它是名詞。例如：

現時考入大學不難。

University <u>entry</u> is not difficult now.

這博物館免費入場。

<u>Entry</u> to the museum is free.

他企圖非法進入該房屋。

He tried to gain illegal <u>entry</u> into the house.

你不可把車駛進有「不得進入」標記的街道。

You must not drive up a street with a No <u>Entry</u> sign.

! NOTES 注意 *!*

英文 infinitive "to" 後面不能連接 entry。例如，"進入該區需要許可證。"，不可以説 ✘ A permit is required to entry to the area.。

3.23 everyday 不等於 every day

近年很多廣告和宣傳小冊子說到「每天、天天」的時候，經常把 every day 錯誤寫成 everyday。這可能是在打字的時候，沒有分開 every 和 day，而電腦的 spell check 也因為 everyday 不是錯字而沒有指出它是不對的。

這錯誤在中國人的社會日漸普遍，例如某蔬菜店的英文名稱本該用 every day，卻用錯了 everyday，大概是因為任何一個略懂英文的人從字面看也會以為 everyday 是「每天、天天」的意思。但我們要學好英文，就連這類看似小的錯誤也要清除，不應混淆 everyday 和 every day，因為 everyday 根本不等於 every day，自然不是「每天、天天」的意思。例如：

午餐時間：每天上午 11 時半至下午 2 時。

    不是 ✘ Lunch: everyday from 11:30 a.m. to 2 p.m.

    而是 ✔ Lunch: every day from 11:30 a.m. to 2 p.m.

其實 everyday 是形容詞，它是「平常、普遍、一般、日常」的意思。由於它是形容詞，它放在名詞前面，修飾名詞，但它不是「每天、天天」的意思。例如：

經常發生的事

everyday occurrence

日常的生活程序

everyday routine

日常英語

everyday English

日常生活

everyday life

日常用紙

everyday paper

所以表示天天新鮮，應是 fresh every day。

「每天、天天」其他的正確例子還有：

我們不會天天都看見蛇。

We don't see snakes every day.

他每天都查詢相同的問題。

He asked the same question every day.

! NOTES 注意 !

我們說「每月、每天晚上、每星期」英文是 every month、every night、every week，不是 everymonth、everynight、everyweek，所以「每天、天天」不是 everyday。

3.24 expire 之後可以用 passive voice 嗎？

在法律和商業文件裏，我們經常說「期滿、到期、屆滿、終止」。例如協議、合約、牌照或保證到期，英語是 <u>expire</u>，它是動詞。以下是錯誤例子：

協議昨天到期。

> ✗ The agreement was <u>expired</u> yesterday.

僱傭合約期滿。

> ✗ The employment contract had been <u>expired</u>.

他的駕駛執照快將期滿。

> ✗ His driving licence will be <u>expired</u>.

保證已經屆滿。

> ✗ The guarantee has been <u>expired</u>.

到底錯在哪裏呢？這是因為大家不知道 <u>expire</u> 是不及物動詞，而不及物動詞後面不接賓語，所以它不能用被動式。

所以上述各句正確答案如下：

> ✓ The agreement <u>expired</u> yesterday.
>
> ✓ The employment contract has <u>expired</u>.
>
> ✓ His driving licence will <u>expire</u>.
>
> ✓ The guarantee has <u>expired</u>.

也許有人以為 expired 是形容詞而説 ✘ Your passport is expired.，但這是不對的，我們應該説 ✔ Your passport expired.。

其他例子還有：

物業租約將在一年後屆滿。

　✔ The lease on the property expires in one year's time.

當我的會籍到期時，我不會續期。

　✔ When my membership expires, I will not renew it.

3.25 following 和 as follows 的差異

我們在各類文件裏經常說「下列」和「下面」，英文除了用 <u>as follows</u> 之外，也可使用 <u>following</u>。但大家不要把它跟 <u>follows</u> 混淆，寫成 ✘ <u>followings</u> 是錯誤的。

! NOTES 注意 !

<u>following</u> 是形容詞、名詞和介詞，它的結尾沒有 s。

錯誤例子如下：

已選出下列人士參加下月的比賽：彼德、大衛和路易士。

> ✘ The <u>followings</u> have been elected to play in the match next month: Peter, David and Louis.

下面是主席演說的摘要。

> ✘ The <u>followings</u> are summaries of the Chairman's speech.

例子列出如下：

> ✘ The examples are listed as <u>followings</u>:

上述句子應改為

> ✔ The <u>following</u> have been elected to play in the match next month: Peter, David and Louis.

> ✔ The <u>following</u> is a summary of the Chairman's speech.

✔ The examples are listed as <u>follows</u>:

另外必須注意的是：following 用作名詞時，它後面的動詞 be 用單數還是複數，取決於後面談及的人或物的單複數。例如：

現綜述如下：

The <u>following</u> is a summary:

己選定下列人員參加：彼德、大衛、威廉和賓。

The <u>following</u> have been chosen to take part: Peter, David, William and Ben.

其他例子還有：

請仔細閱讀如下：

Please read the <u>following</u> carefully:

下面是我的全名。

The <u>following</u> is my full name.

下面是我們的全名。

The <u>following</u> are our full names.

我們與 ABC 公司的協議條款如下：

The <u>following</u> are the terms and conditions of our agreement with ABC Company：

3.26 forget 後跟 to 或 ing 有不同意思

大家學習英語動詞語法時，相信記得有些動詞會後接不定式 (infinitive to)，其他會後接現在分詞 (present participle) 即 ing 形式，成為動名詞 (gerund)。但最麻煩的是有些動詞既可後接不定式，又可後接現在分詞。這類動詞後接不定式或現在分詞時，兩者意思會完全不同，所以容易導致犯錯。

以 forget 為例：forget + to 與 forget + ing 的意思最難區分。例如：

不要忘記簽名。

　　不是 ✘ Don't forget signing your name.

　　而是 ✔ Don't forget to sign your name.

他忘記鎖門。

　　不是 ✘ He forgot locking the door.

　　而是 ✔ He forgot to lock the door.

為甚麼呢？

　　因為 Don't forget signing your name.

　　　　是「不要忘記你已經簽名」的意思。

　　He forgot locking his door.

　　　　是「他忘記門已經上鎖」的意思。

簡單來說， <u>forget</u> + to 是「忘記做一件未做的事」，
而 <u>forget</u> + ing 是「做了一件事，卻不記得」。

其他例子還有：

不要忘記帶錢包。

Don't <u>forget</u> to bring your wallet.

我永遠不會忘記在山頂找到的那個男孩子。

I'll never <u>forget</u> finding that boy at the peak.

他永遠不會忘記第一次看到的殺人鯨。

He would never <u>forget</u> seeing the killer whale for the first time.

我幾乎忘記邀請瑪麗。

I nearly <u>forgot</u> to invite Mary.

3.27「最近」用 last 還是 the last？

last 是「最後一個」的意思。以下是「最後一個」的正確例子：

他趕上最後一班的公共汽車回家。

✔ He caught the last bus home.

我們的房子是右邊最盡頭的那棟。

✔ Our house is the last house on the right.

會議在一月最後一個星期舉行。

✔ The meeting was held in the last week of January.

這是最後一次董事會會議。

✔ This is the last board meeting.

但是因 last 也是「最近、上一個」的意思，所以很多時候大家沒法區分它們。

last 正確使用的例子：

我們昨晚／上星期一／上星期／上月／去年夏天／去年在沙田遇見他們。

✔ We saw them last night / Monday / week / month / summer / year in Shatin.

謝謝你最近的來信。

✔ Thanks for your last letter.

他們去年的選舉表現得很差。

✔ They did badly in <u>last</u> year's election.

區議會在上次會議提出一項新設計。

✔ The district council proposed a new design at its <u>last</u> meeting.

該項目於去年夏天結束。

✔ The project ended in <u>last</u> summer.

! NOTES 注意 *!*

記着 last 前面有 the 的時候，它是「最後一個」的意思。前面沒有 the 的時候，它是「最近的、上一個」的意思。此外，要注意以下特別用法：The <u>last</u> thing he needed was more money. 是「他最不需要的就是更多的錢。」; She is the <u>last</u> person he would trust. 是「她是他最不能信任的人。」。

3.28 注意特殊動詞的時式變化

相信大家都知道，英文 not 用於把詞或語句變為相反意思，並經常與動詞連用，以表達「否定、不是」的意思。

如果句子裏有助動詞（auxiliary verbs）如 be、do 或情態助動詞（modal auxiliary verbs）如 will、shall、would、should、can、could、may、might、must 和 ought，在 not 後面，我們應該用動詞的基本形式。例如：

他們不回答。

They did not answer.

她日語説得不好。

She does not speak Japanese very well.

我不喜歡它。

I do not like it.

但是，只有在進行式（progressive 或 continuous）句子裏，即在 be 動詞（如 is、am、are、was、were、will / shall be、has / have been 等）後面，我們才會把動詞變為 ing 形式。有沒有 not 也一樣。例如：

我在做蛋糕。

I am making a cake.

蘇珊一直學習韓語多年。

Susan has been trying to learn Korean for years.

他不來。

He is not coming.

我們不留下來。

We are not staying.

以下是錯誤例子：

不要躺在地上。

✘ Do not lying.

應改為：

✔ Do not lie down.

✔ Do not lie on the ground.

其他例子還有：

仰臥 / 側臥 / 俯臥

Lie on your back / side / front

臥牀

Lie in bed

躺在沙灘上

Lie on a beach

! NOTES 注意 *!*

lie 的時式變化如下：現在式 lie；過去式 lay；過去分詞 lain。

3.29 認識被動式的使用原則

如果要表達「門已鎖上」的意思，許多人會犯錯，以下是錯誤的例子：

✘ The door has locked.

出錯主要是因為大家不知道這句應該使用被動式。但怎知道某個動詞可以使用被動式呢？或應該甚麼時候使用被動式呢？

原來英語裏只有及物動詞 (transitive verbs) 可以使用被動式及主動式。不及物動詞 (intransitive verbs) 只可以使用主動式。所謂及物動詞，是指它後面一定接賓語或作為賓語的片語。

因此，應改為：

✔ The door has been locked.

在一般英語詞典，都會說明某個動詞是及物動詞還是不及動詞。有些詞典用 T 或 t 來表示它是及物動詞，用 I 或 i 來表示它是及物動詞。例如：

sell 是 (I; T) 表示它既是不及物動詞，也是及物動詞。例如：

如果你願意出售的話，我想買你的車。

I would like to buy your car if you are willing to sell.

她正在考慮賣掉房子。

She is thinking of selling her house.

這本雜誌賣十元。

The magazine sells for / at $10.

又例如：

commence 和 increase (I; T)，表示它們既是不及物動詞，也是及物動詞。

會議現在就開始。

The meeting may now commence.

我們現在可以開會了。

We may now commence the meeting.

這個城鎮的人口增加了。

The population of this town has increased.

他們把石油價格提高了百分十。

They have increased the price of petrol by 10%.

但由於很多人沒有查閱英語詞典，也忽略被動式的使用規則，因而出現了胡亂使用被動式的情況。即是説我們很容易在應該使用被動式時，沒有使用被動式。但在不應該使用時，卻用了被動式。例如：

這本書銷路很好。

不是 ✘ The book is sold wells.

而是 ✔ The book sells well.

行動開始。

不是 ✘ The operation has been commenced.

而是 ✔ The operation has commenced.

房間的溫度上升了。

不是 ✘ The room temperature has been increased.

而是 ✔ The room temperature has increased.

請記着：increase 和 decrease、decline 可以用主動或被動式，但通常用主動式。例如：

電油價格降低了 10%。

不是 ✘ The price of petrol has been decreased by 10 per cent.

而是 ✔ The price of petrol has decreased by 10 per cent.

又例如 rise 和 fall，它們是不及物動詞，所以只用主動式，不用被動式。例如：

我們的營業額上升了兩千萬元。

Our turnover has risen by over $20 million.

上月遊客的數目下降了 5 %。

The number of tourists declined by 5 per cent last month.

3.30 字尾有沒有 s 會使 minute 和 agenda 含義不同

任何機構都會經常舉行會議，而正式會議一定需要會議記錄。會議記錄的英文是 minutes，但很多人也許由於時間緊逼或一時大意，無論是題目或內容裏的 minutes 都經常漏了 s，變成 minute。因為已通過的會議記錄是正式文件，並且可能會保存多年與會者在任何時間都會看見這錯誤，除了影響部門或機構的形象，還會反映相關人員工作不夠認真。以下是正確例子：

會議結束後，主席仔細閱讀會議記錄。

The Chairman went over the <u>minutes</u> when the meeting was over.

每次會議記錄的草擬本將會在隨後的會議上通過作實。

The draft <u>minutes</u> of every meeting will be confirmed at the subsequent meeting.

另外，召開會議前需要議事日程或議程，英文是 <u>agenda</u>，指會議上需要討論或考慮的項目清單，注意 <u>agenda</u> 是單數，除非是指多個會議各自的議程，否則它是沒有複數形式 <u>agendas</u> 的。會議中多項或不同議程的英文是 <u>agenda</u> items。例如：

你看了第二次及第三次會議的議程嗎？

Have you read the <u>agendas</u> of the second and third meetings?

秘書把財政問題放在議程的第一項。

The Secretary put finance at the top of the <u>agenda</u>.

一小時後我們仍在討論議程上的第二項。

After one hour, we were still discussing the second item on the <u>agenda</u>.

他只留在會議上討論最先的兩項議程。

He only stayed for the first two <u>agenda</u> items.

議程中有幾個重要的項目。

There were several important <u>agenda</u> items.

他們在三個議程上達成一致意見。

They achieved agreement on the three <u>agenda</u> items.

此外，複數的 agendas 是抽象用法，指「意圖、目的或議題」，即「待辦事項或待解決問題」。例如：

因意圖不同，他們勢必發生衝突。

They are bound to clash as they have different <u>agendas</u>.

這些政策議題大部份隸屬於局方。

These policy <u>agendas</u> lie mostly under the department.

3.31 look forward to 後跟動名詞

在一般商業信件裏一個常見錯誤是：

　　✘ <u>Look forward to</u> see you soon.

因為 <u>look forward to</u> 裏的 to 是介詞，所以後面要用名詞。例如：

我盼望着過週末。

　　I <u>am looking forward to</u> the weekend.

如果後面是動詞，就要用動名詞 (gerund)。

故此，應改為：

　　✔ <u>Look forward to</u> seeing you soon.

即使是 I <u>am looking forward to</u> 後面也是用 seeing you soon。

其他例子還有：

我一心盼望參加你的派對。

　　I <u>am looking forward to</u> going to your party.

我盼望七天內收到你客戶的支票。

　　I <u>look forward to</u> receiving your client's cheque within 7 days.

我期望下星期探望瑪麗。

　　I <u>look forward to</u> visiting Mary next week.

我們期望下個月前往北極。

　　We <u>are looking forward to</u> going to the North Pole next month.

3.32 撰寫會議記錄時，注意轉述時間要用 the

在進行會議時，我們經常提及將來要做的事情的時間，例如「次天、第二天」next day、「下個星期」next week、「下個月」next month、「下一個秋天」next autumn 和「下一年、明年」next year 等。但我們對上述時間撰寫會議記錄時，卻不能這樣說，必須加上 the，因為 the next 是用在過去時間的陳述句或間接引語，是指該時間由會議當時所說的實際時間開始計算，不是指會議紀錄當天的時間，所以不用 the 是不對的。正確例子如下：

他們同意下一天見面。

　✓ They agreed to meet the next day.

我們應可在下個月之內收到報告。

　✓ We should receive the report within the next month.

我期望接下來的一個星期會有些改變。

　✓ I expected that some changes would be made in the next week.

將會在明年內向委員會提出建議。

　✓ The proposal would be put forward to the committee within the next year.

希望下月採取行動。

✔ It was hoped that action would be taken the <u>next</u> month.

使用 <u>next</u> 的正確例子：

明年我將去那裏。

✔ I shall go there <u>next</u> week.

下星期五我們會去釣魚。

✔ <u>Next</u> Friday we are going fishing.

下月九日將會召開聆訊。

✔ On the 9th of <u>next</u> month, a hearing will be conducted.

我們可能在明年查詢同一個問題。

✔ We may ask the same question <u>next</u> year.

! *NOTES* 注意 !

在直接引語或敘述句，next 前面不用介詞如 on、in 或 at 等。例如：
我們下個月去日本。
不是 ✘ We will go to Japan in <u>next</u> month.
而是 ✔ We will go to Japan <u>next</u> month.

next

3.33 小心分辨 and 和 or

相信大家在學校的教室、公司的會議室甚至一些商店都會看過
「不准飲食 *No eating and drinking」的告示，但問題是「不准飲
食」的英文不是 *No eating and drinking，說 *No food and drink
也不好。這錯誤我幾十年前已經發現，可惜到了今天它仍然存
在。事實上，多年來我希望大家努力糾正錯誤的英語，就是因
為錯誤的英語會產生惡性循環。那麼 *No eating and drinking
為甚麼不對呢？

首先我們要知道，在英語裏，凡提及兩個或以上的選擇或可能
性時我們會用 <u>or</u>。因此不准飲食應改為：

不准飲食

   ✘ No eating and drinking.

   ✘ No food and drink.

   ✔ No eating <u>or</u> drinking.

   ✔ No food <u>or</u> drink.

另一方面，從字面上看，No eating and drinking 是表示「飲和
食不可以一起」，但「單獨飲、單獨食」就可以。這當然不是原
來的意思。

其他例子還有：

你要些茶或咖啡嗎？

   Would you like some tea <u>or</u> coffee?

是男孩還是女孩？

Is it a boy or a girl?

它可能是黑、白或灰的。

It can be black, white or grey.

另外，在否定句，or 是用來提及兩種或多種事物。例如：

她不會讀、不會寫。

She can't read or write.

很多人既無房屋、又無工作、又無家庭。

There are many people without houses, jobs or family.

他們沒水、沒食物，所以很快死亡。

They were going to die because they had no water or food.

她不認識任何編輯、也不認識任何作家。

She did not know any editors or writers.

我不喜歡豬和牛肉。

I do not like pork or beef.

3.34 note 沒有被動式

日常電郵裏，*Please be noted that 這錯誤像 *Please be reported that 一樣普遍。大家經常用它，卻不知道是錯的。

note 可以當「注意、留意」的意思。例如：

請注意這賬單必須在七天之內付款。

Please note that this bill must be paid within 7 days.

請注意我們星期日不營業。

Please note (that) we will be closed on Sunday.

他留意有人在跟蹤他。

He noted that someone was following him.

為甚麼不可以説 *Please be noted that 呢？這是因為 Please 開頭的句子是祈使句，主語 you 省略了。我們只可以説 Please note that ... 。 説 *Please be noted that ... 是「請被注意」，但意思就是不通，別人不知道你想説甚麼。

當然，我們可以改説 Please be advised ...「謹通知你」或 Please advise「請惠賜卓見」這兩句語法都對，但説來有點文縐縐，屬於比較古老的英語，也是較正式的用法。現在我們多用 Let us know（口語常用）或 Please tell us ... 。例如：

有任何問題就告訴我們。

Let us know if you have any questions.

有任何困難就告訴我們。

Please tell us if you have any problems.

我們能幫助甚麼，只管說。

Let us know how we can help.

請告訴我們你打算甚麼時候到。

Let us know what time you are planning to arrive.

跟我們講講面試怎麼樣。

Let us know what happened at the interview.

工程完成時請告訴我們。

Please tell us when the works will be completed.

3.35 occur 不接賓語，也不能用被動式

這是錯誤使用被動式的另一個常見例子。有關「被動式」passive voice 的詳細解釋見 expire 及 lock 兩章。

首先，因為 occur 是「不及物動詞」intransitive verb，所以它不接賓語，也不能使用被動式。以下是錯誤例子：

這事是何時發生的？

不是 ✘ When was the incident occurred?

而是 ✔ When did the incident occur?

剛發生了出乎意料的事。

不是 ✘ Something unexpected has just been occurred.

而是 ✔ Something unexpected has occurred.

其他正確例子還有：

許多意外死亡在家裏發生。

Many accidental deaths occur at home.

爆炸在晚上七時發生。

The explosion occurred at 7 p.m.

她説頭痛只在夜裏出現。

She said that her headaches occurred at nights only.

意外在三個月前發生。

The accident <u>occurred</u> 3 months ago.

另外，意思和 <u>occur</u> 一樣的 <u>happen</u> 也是「不及物動詞」，只用「主動式」，不可以使用「被動式」。由於它在日常英語較 <u>occur</u> 常用，請大家正確使用，例如：

意外是在他工作時發生的。

The accident <u>happened</u> while he was at work.

我不知道這是怎麼發生的。

I don't know how this <u>happened</u>.

今天家裏發生了有趣的事。

Funny things <u>happened</u> at home today.

! NOTES 注意 *!*

請留意容易產生類似錯誤的其他詞語還有 seem、result from / in、appear / disappear、belong、depend 和 arrive 等，它們都是只有「主動式」，沒有「被動式」。

3.36 improve 不可與 problem 搭配使用

日常英語裏我們愛說 improve，它是「改善、改進、提高或變好」的意思。例如：

我想改善 / 提高我的英語水平。

I want to <u>improve</u> my English.

他們希望星期日之前天氣會變好。

They hope the weather <u>improves</u> before Sunday.

他為改善辦公室職員的工作條件做了許多工作。

He did a lot to <u>improve</u> conditions for the office staff.

改善 / 提高表現

<u>improve</u> performance

改善 / 提高生活質素

<u>improve</u> quality of life

還有其他例子：

<u>improve</u> our vocabulary / understanding of world affairs / habits / marks in school 等等

但大家請注意：中文常說的「改善問題」，英文不是 <u>improve</u>

the problem。為甚麼呢？中文裏可以說「改善問題」，但英文的 problem 是不可以 improve 的。這是搭配問題，就像中文說「學習知識」，但英文沒有 learn knowledge，因為英語 knowledge 不是 learn 的，那是直譯或硬譯，「學習知識」的英語是 acquire 或 gain knowledge 或簡單地說 learn 就可以。事實上，英語 learn 已是 get knowledge or skills 的意思，所以無須說 learn knowledge。

! NOTES 注意 !

記着 improve 的中文解釋是「使～變得更好」。常見搭配詞是：situation / condition 情況、health 健康等。

至於 improve，我們記着它的英文解釋就明白：Improve refers to any means of making something higher in quality or more desirable in nature. 所以我們不能說 improve the problem。

那麼「改善問題」的正確英語是甚麼呢？正確的說法是：reduce the problem，例如：

他們嘗試改善貧窮問題。

They are trying to reduce the problem of poverty.

我們必須改善交通擠塞問題。

We must reduce the problem of traffic congestion.

! NOTES 注意 !

在正確搭配方面，英文有 solve / overcome / settle / tackle / deal with / handle / address the problem，即解決 / 克服或處理問題。

3.37 remember 搭配 to 或 ing 產生不同含義

相信大家學會了某些動詞如 forget 既可連接不定式，又可連接現在分詞成為動名詞 (gerund)。由於這類動詞的使用會造成不同意思，而且不容易明白，所以現在再以 remember 多解釋一次。

我們知道 remember 是「想起、記得」的意思。但 remember + to 與 remember + ing 的意思不同。

> **記得簽名。**
>
> 不是 ✘ <u>Remember</u> signing your name.
>
> 而是 ✓ <u>Remember</u> to sign your name.

> **他想到要鎖門。**
>
> 不是 ✘ He <u>remembered</u> locking the door.
>
> 而是 ✓ He <u>remembered</u> to lock the door.

上述例子為甚麼是錯的呢？

因為 <u>Remember</u> signing your name. 是「記得你已經簽名。」的意思。而 He <u>remembered</u> locking his door. 是「他想到門已上鎖。」的意思。

簡單來説，<u>remember</u> + to 是「記得做一件未做的事」，而 <u>remember</u> + ing 是「想到做了一件事」。

其他例子還有：

記得帶錢包。

Remember to bring your wallet.

我記不起借了錢給他。

I don't remember lending him the money.

他永遠記不起已經澆了花。

He never remembers watering the plants.

記得交罰款。

Remember to pay the fine.

我記得把信寄了。

I remember posting the letter.

3.38 report 用作及物或不及物動詞有不同含義

每天傳來傳去的文件或電郵裏經常出現一些常見錯誤，以訛傳訛，久而久之人人以為那錯誤是正確的，Please be <u>reported</u> that 就是其中一個例子。

很多人會説，<u>report</u> 是「報告」，「我要向你報告」不就是 Please be <u>reported</u> 嗎？但這樣的用法是不對的，為甚麼呢？

這是因為 <u>report</u> 用作「報告、報導、報知、記述、敘述」的意思時，它是不及物動詞，後面不接名詞。例如：

他沒甚麼可報告的。

He had nothing to <u>report</u>.

她説她病了。

She <u>reported</u> sick.

但當它用作「告發、被人報告」的意思時，它是及物動詞，後面可接名詞。例如：

她向校長告發了這個男孩（在校舍內吸煙）。

She <u>reported</u> the boy to the principal (for smoking on the school premises).

任何罪案均應馬上向警方報告。

Any case of crime should be <u>reported</u> immediately to the police.

據說有人在中環見到她了。

She is <u>reported</u> to have been seen in Central.

你因超速被人檢舉。

You were <u>reported</u> to the police for speeding.

! NOTES 注意 *!*

請記着 *Please be reported 是個祈使句，主語是 you ，也就是 *You are reported... 。變成：「你被人告發某件事……」而不是「我要向你報告……」。收到電郵的人應該會啼笑皆非。

會議推遲至星期一上午十一時舉行。

不是 ✘ Please be <u>reported</u> that the meeting will be postponed to 11 a.m. on Monday.

而是 ✔ Please be <u>informed</u> that the meeting will be postponed to 11 a.m. on Monday.

或是 ✔ The meeting will be <u>postponed</u> to 11 a.m. on Monday.

其他例子還有：

他每星期必須向警方報到。

He has to <u>report</u> to the police every week.

他們早上九時上班。

They <u>report</u> for work at 9 a.m.

3.39 reply 之後不可加 me

日常文件或電郵、Whatsapp 和微信經常出現 *Please reply me. 或 *Reply me. 的錯誤，它們是中文「請覆我、覆我」的直譯，但問題是這兩句無需用 me。

為甚麼 reply 後面加上 me 是不對呢？這是因為在英文語法規則裏，reply 用作動詞時不帶賓語（object），因它是「不及物動詞」（intransitive verbs），詞典多用 v.i. 或 i 來表示。要帶賓語時就要加 to。

其他正確例子還有：

他問她到哪裏去但她不回答。

He asked her where she was going but she didn't reply.

你回覆了她的信沒有？

Have you replied to her letter?

她從來沒給我回過信。

She never replied to any of my letters.

我們的廣告收到許多回覆。

We had a lot of replies to our advertisement.

他不給我回答他問題的機會。

He gave me no chance to reply to his question.

3.40 注意 succeed 不可後跟不定式 to

尋找工作時，寫了求職信申請某職位後，經過筆試或面試，如果不成功的話，可能會收到回信，通常是「謝謝你申請上述職位，很遺憾你不獲聘用。」Thank you for your application for the above position. We regret to inform you that you have not been selected for appointment. 。但有些公司可能會加上 *You were not succeeded. 或 *You were not success. ，但這兩句都是錯的，「你不成功」應改用 You are not successful. 。

為甚麼呢？這是因為英文 <u>succeed</u> 是動詞，而 <u>success</u> 是名詞。它們的形容詞是 <u>successful</u> 。

首先， <u>succeed</u> 是「不及物動詞」，它不帶賓語。例如：

他差一點就成功。

He almost <u>succeeded</u>.

治療沒有成功。

The therapy <u>did not succeed</u>.

計劃完成得十分成功。

The plan <u>succeeded</u> pretty well.

它也可加介詞 in 和動名詞 (in + ing) ，但不能帶不定式 to。例如：

他們成功籌集一百萬元。

They <u>succeeded</u> in raising $1 million.

她贏了選舉。

She <u>succeeded</u> in winning the election.

用形容詞 <u>successful</u> 的例子：

針對非法勞工的行動很成功。

The operation against illegal workers was <u>successful</u>.

彼德是個非常成功的政治家。

Peter was a very <u>successful</u> politician.

其他例子還有：

我們嘗試和她聯絡但沒有成功。

We tried to contact her, but without <u>success</u>.

這計劃非常成功。

The plan was a great <u>success</u>.

我們已經基本上實現了目標。

We have largely <u>succeeded</u> in our aims.

! NOTES 注意 !

succeed 不能後跟不定詞，一定要用介詞 in 來後接動名詞或名詞。
be successful 後接 –ing 動詞。

3.41 不要混淆 temporary 和 temporarily

任何機構、辦公室和大廈裏，很多服務或設施都因某些原因暫停運作。「停止」的英文是 suspend，但不少告示在它前面加 <u>temporary</u>，成為 *<u>temporary</u> suspended，那是不對的。

造成這個錯誤，原因也許是忘記了基本的語法規則，我們應記着 suspend 是動詞，所以應該用副詞來修飾它。在上述例子，<u>temporary</u> 是形容詞，它一般用來修飾名詞而不是動詞。例如：

暫時的挫折

<u>temporary</u> setback

臨時工

<u>temporary</u> jobs

臨時安排

<u>temporary</u> arrangement

而 <u>temporary</u> 的副詞是 <u>temporarily</u>，它可以用來修飾 suspend。例如：

每天飛往東京的航班暫停。

The daily flight to Tokyo has been <u>temporarily</u> suspended.

我們很抱歉列車暫停服務。

We regret train service is <u>temporarily</u> unavailable.

這個辦事處暫時關閉進行裝修。

This office is closed <u>temporarily</u> for decoration.

電話暫時失靈。

The telephone is <u>temporarily</u> out of order.

他們暫時受阻。

They were <u>temporarily</u> delayed.

3.42 不要混淆 ed 和 ing 形容詞

像 terrified 和 terrifying 這類出自同一來源的形容詞 (見以下更多的例子),它們很容易因為混淆而產生錯誤。

請記着:當一個人説出自己的感覺就要用 ed 的形容詞;即句子開頭是人,例子 Peter、David、Mary、he、she is / was... 或 I am / was... 或 you, we, they are / were... 等我們就要用有 ed 結尾的形容詞。例如 excited, bored...

但當事物或東西、事情或事件令人有某種感覺的時候,我們就要用有 ing 結尾的形容詞。例如 exciting, boring...

以下是更多例子:

annoyed	annoying
astonished	astonishing
bored	boring
confused	confusing
disappointed	disappointing
disgusted	disgusting
excited	exciting
frightened	frightening
interested	interesting

pleased	pleasing
satisfied	satisfying
scared	scaring
shocked	shocking
surprised	surprising
tired	tiring
worried	worrying

例如：

我們很悶 / 那堂課很沉悶。

We are bored / The lecture was boring.

他很興奮 / 那電影很緊張刺激。

He is excited / The film was exciting.

她很累 / 那工作很累人。

She is very tired / The work is very tiring.

彼德受驚了 / 那蛇很嚇人。

Peter is frightened / The snake was frightening.

我很失望 / 他的成績令人失望。

I am disappointed / His results are disappointing.

3.43 謝謝到來不是 Thank you for your coming.

在一般應用文裏，我們常常説「謝謝你的合作、謝謝你的幫忙、謝謝你的耐性、謝謝你的所有工作、謝謝支持、謝謝你的迅速回應」等。

以上各句的英語是

Thank you for your cooperation.

Thank you for your help.

Thank you for your patience.

Thank you for all your work.

Thank you for your support.

Thank you for your prompt reply.

但説到「謝謝到來」，我們不説 Thank you for your coming. 因為我們説 your coming 是累贅了。

應説 Thank you for coming.

Thanks for = Thank you for，是口語化表達形式。

注意 Thank you 較 thanks 正式一點。

但我們不能説

✘ Thank your cooperation.

✘ Thank your help.

✗ Thank your patience.

✗ Thank all your work.

✗ Thank your support.

✗ Thank your prompt reply.

在以上例子，沒有 you for 是不對的。

其他例子還有：

那婆婆感謝該警員幫她橫過馬路。

The old woman thanked the policeman for helping her cross the road.

感謝聆聽。

Thank you for listening.

謝謝你的意見。

Thank you for your advice.

感謝你們的發言。

Thanks for your speeches.

詞性混淆

4.1 **If you are indoor 是錯誤的**

在任何公共場所裏，我們都會接觸到「室內、戶內」及「室外、戶外」這些中文詞彙，英語是 indoor 和 outdoor。但很多時我們很容易忽略了它們與 <u>indoors</u> 及 outdoors 的區別。簡單來說，indoor 和 outdoor 是形容詞，即它們修飾名詞。indoors 及 outdoors 則是副詞，即它們修飾動詞、形容詞及其他副詞。例如：

戶內／戶外工作

　　不是 ✘ indoors / outdoors work

　　而是 ✔ indoor / outdoor work

在室內／室外工作

　　不是 ✘ work indoor / outdoor

　　而是 ✔ work <u>indoors</u> / outdoors

在戶內及戶外生活

　　不是 ✘ spend our lives indoor and outdoor

　　而是 ✔ spend our lives <u>indoors</u> and outdoors

他喜歡室內／室外活動。

　　不是 ✘ He likes indoors and outdoors activities.

　　而是 ✔ He likes indoor and outdoor activities.

室內不准吸煙。

　　不是 ✘ No smoking indoor is allowed.

而是 ✔ No smoking <u>indoors</u> is allowed.

如果你在室外……

不是 ✘ If you are outdoor...

而是 ✔ If you are outdoors...

其他正確例子還有：

應讓他們每天戶外活動一小時。

They should be given access to the outdoors for one hour each day.

它是一項專為 60 歲或以上長者而設的嶄新戶外支援服務。

It is a brand new outdoor support service for the elderly aged 60 or above.

所有室內工作及公共場所應該禁煙。

All indoor workplaces and public places should be smoke free.

下雨時請進入室內。

Go <u>indoors</u> when it begins to rain.

4.2 「證實死亡」用 die 的過去分詞還是名詞？

相信在商界、教育界、醫護界和紀律部隊工作的朋友都非常熟悉 <u>certify</u> 這個詞語，它是「證明、證實、審核、核證、核實」的意思。例如：

這些賬目經核數師審核無誤。

The accounts were <u>certified</u> correct by an auditor.

他們需要核實工程是否完成得令人滿意。

They need to <u>certify</u> that the works have been satisfactorily completed.

我證明這是真正的副本。

I <u>certify</u> that this is a true copy.

茲證明陳勞倫先生在二零 XX 年三月一日至二零 XX 年四月十二日期間於本公司任職。

This is to <u>certify</u> that Mr. Lawrence Chan was in our employ from 1 March 20XX to 12 April 20XX.

這份文件被核證為真文本。

The document is <u>certified</u> as a true copy.

認證副本

<u>certified</u> copy

經銀行證明可兑現的支票

　　<u>certified</u> cheque

實證病人

　　<u>certified</u> patient

! *NOTES* 注意 !

在任何意外現場或醫院，傷者或病人很多時被證實死亡，有關人員都會簡略説 "cert" 咗，或 <u>certified</u>，即 He / she was <u>certified</u>.。但全句該是 He was <u>certified</u> dead. 而不是 ✘ He was <u>certified</u> death.

因為 <u>certify</u> somebody dead 的意思是 when a doctor says officially that a person is dead。病人被證實死亡，<u>certify</u> 要用被動式，成為 He was <u>certified</u> dead.。

其他例子還有：

司機被證實當場死亡。

　　The driver was <u>certified</u> dead at the scene.

她送院時已被證實死亡。

　　She was <u>certified</u> dead on arrival to the hospital.

2002 年這專輯在美國被認證為金唱片。

　　This album was <u>certified</u> gold in the United States in 2002.

4.3 「生效」不是 with effective from

無論是政府機構或部門，以至任何商業機構、公司或企業，在處理日常事務或一般業務的文件裏，經常說到「生效、實行、實施」這類詞語。英文很多時可以用 effect 或 effective，前者是名詞，後者是形容詞。例如：

新管制措施將在明年起實施。

The new controls will come / be brought / be put into effect next year.

新制度將在下星期一開始實行。

The new system will take effect next Monday.

新速度限制何時生效？

When does the new speed limit become effective?

合同條款將在七月一日生效。

The terms of the contract will take effect / come into effect from 1 July.

價格由五月一日起增加 10％。

Prices are increased 10% with effect from 1 May.

利率已經削減，由下月初開始生效。

Interest rates have been cut with effect from the beginning of next month.

但很多時我們會混淆 effect 和 effective。例如：

她辭職，即時生效。

不是 ✘ She is resigning from the post with immediate effective.

而是 ✔ She is resigning from the post with immediate <u>effect</u>.

這些建議即將付諸實行。

不是 ✘ The recommendations will soon be put into effective.

而是 ✔ The recommendations will soon be put into <u>effect</u>.

由 2018 年 5 月 25 日生效。

不是 ✘ With effective from 25th May 2018.

而是 ✔ With <u>effect</u> from 25th May 2018.

協議由十二月一日起生效。

不是 ✘ The agreement will become effect from 1st December.

而是 ✔ The agreement will become <u>effective</u> from 1st December.

4.4 「先到先得」不是 first come, first serve

「先到先得」是常用語，不過許多人用英文表達時，serve 不小心漏了 d，寫成 ✗ first come, first serve，這是不對的。即使是 ✗ on a first-come, first-serve basis 或 ✗ on a first-come-first-serve basis 也是錯的，必須寫成 ✔ on a first-come, first-served basis 或 ✔ on a first-come-first-served basis 才對。正確例子如下：

他們首天出售一百元的門票 —— 先到先得。

✔ They sell $100 tickets on the first day – first come, first served.

現時可供應十個露營地點，先到先得。

✔ There are ten camp sites available on a first-come, first-served basis.

入場券先到先得，售完即止。

✔ Admission tickets are available on first come, first served basis.

申請不會以先到先得方式處理。

✔ Applications will not be processed on a first-come-first-served basis.

下列例子都是錯誤的：

免費門票先到先得。

✘ Free tickets will be available *first come, first serve.*

規則或做法都是講求先到先得。

✘ "<u>First come, first serve</u>" is also the rule and standard practice.

很難以先到先得方式處理申請。

✘ It is difficult to determine the applications on "<u>first-come-first-serve</u>" basis.

座位分配將不以先到先得方式分配。

✘ Seats will not be allocated on a <u>first come first serve</u> basis.

另外必須注意 <u>first come, first served</u> 可以加上連字符號寫成 <u>first-come-first-served</u>，但不可混合兩者隨便使用。例如：

✘ <u>first come-first served</u>

✘ <u>first-come first-served</u>

4.5 「即時上班」不是 immediate available

香港工商業發達，各行各業分秒必爭，許多僱主不想人手短缺影響生產力，經常希望新聘請的員工能夠即時上班，所以招聘廣告經常說 *immediate available。

但說 *immediate available 是錯誤的。

由於涉及英語形容詞和副詞運用的基本規則，因此希望大家能夠牢記它為甚麼是錯誤的。

其實，學習英語詞彙最有效的方法是查閱詞典，先看看那個詞彙的詞性是甚麼，從而知道它的運用規則。我們再參考詞典裏的例子，抄寫在筆記簿裏，將來就懂得怎樣運用了。

像上述的 *immediate available，是說應徵人士需要即時上班，即「you are... 或 you should be 即時上班」，所以在後面加上形容詞 available 來表達上班沒有問題，但把 immediate 放在 available 前面就有問題，為甚麼呢？

因為除非我們需要用兩個或以上的形容詞修飾後面的名詞，否則不應隨便連用兩個形容詞，更何況這裏的 immediate 是用來修飾 available 的，所以應該把 immediate 改為副詞 immediately，這正是副詞其中的一個功用：修飾形容詞。

因此，「即時上班」的英文是 ✔ immediately available。

其他錯誤例子還有：

他的提問要點可能不是即時就能看出來的。

✘ The point of his question may not be immediate apparent.

這件事的原因可能不會馬上明朗。

✘ The reasons for this may not be immediate obvious.

新法例即時生效。

✘ The new law will become effective immediate.

正確例子如下：

並非所有活動能夠即時量化。

✔ All activities are not immediately quantifiable.

馬上需要對這苦難負責的人就是主席。

✔ The man immediately responsible for this misery is the chairman.

甚麼是馬上需要報告的意外及受傷？

✔ What are immediately reportable accidents and injuries?

4.6 lack 用作動詞或名詞時的差異

日常生活裏我們最愛說「缺乏」，英文常用詞是 lack，例如缺乏時間 (time)、睡眠 (sleep)、慾望 (desire)、方向 (direction)、熱心 (enthusiasm)、興趣 (interest)、練習 (practice)、資料 (information) 和溝通 (communication)。至於在職場上，我們也經常聽到缺乏經驗 (experience)、信心 (confidence)、知識 (knowledge)、智慧 (wisdom) 和信念 (conviction)。但雖然 lack 很常用，不少人都會用錯。例如：

他缺乏經驗。

不是 ✘ He is <u>lack</u> of experience.

而是 ✔ He has a <u>lack</u> of experience.

或是 ✔ He <u>lacks</u> experience.

產生錯誤的原因是大家不知道 <u>lack</u> 可以是名詞或動詞。

如果我們把它用作名詞，就應該說 He has a <u>lack</u> of ...，例如：

他缺乏信心。

不是 ✘ He <u>lacks</u> of confidence.

而是 ✔ He has a <u>lack</u> of confidence.

當然，最簡單是我們把 <u>lack</u> 用作動詞：She <u>lacks</u> ...，例如：

她缺乏睡眠。

不是 ✘ She is <u>lack</u> of sleep.

而是 ✔ She <u>lacks</u> sleep.

其他例子還有：

許多人缺乏生活的基本必需品。

Many people <u>lack</u> the basic necessities of life.

他們完全缺乏良心。

They completely <u>lack</u> conscience.

這個夏天非常缺水 / 缺乏雨水。

There was a great <u>lack</u> of water / rain this summer.

其他用法還有：

當時缺乏好的食物。

Good food <u>was lacking</u>.

他不缺乏智慧。

He <u>is not lacking</u> in wisdom.

4.7 注意有些形容詞不可直接放在名詞、動名詞之後

近年來，雖然有關中式英語的討論很多，但是還有很多這類錯誤出現。除了 reply me 和 wait me 之外，<u>necessary</u> 也是常犯的錯誤，像 possible、impossible、easy、difficult 和 convenient 一樣，necessary 雖然是形容詞，但不可以直接放在名詞或人稱代名詞和動名詞的後面。錯誤例子如下：

學校需每年進行評估。

✘ Schools are <u>necessary</u> to conduct evaluations every year.

他必須離開。

✘ He is <u>necessary</u> to leave.

我不可能在六時來。

✘ I am <u>impossible</u> to come at six o'clock.

木屋很容易着火。

✘ Wooden huts are <u>easy</u> to catch fire.

成人很難學好英語。

✘ Adults are <u>difficult</u> to learn English well.

你方便看他嗎？

✘ Are you <u>convenient</u> to see him?

造成這些錯誤的原因，主要是大家不熟悉這些形容詞的用法。此外，就是大家習慣用中文對號入座，把中文同樣解釋的英文放在同一位置，以為這是正確用法。總之，necessary、difficult、possible、dangerous、convenient 等形容詞在句子中是不能用人作為主語。

現在請大家看看 necessary 的正確用法：

學校需每年進行評估。

- ✔ Schools need to conduct evaluations every year 或
- ✔ It is necessary for schools to conduct evaluations every year。

食物是生活必須的。

- ✔ Food is necessary for life.

我是不是必須參加這個會議？

- ✔ Is it necessary for me to attend this meeting?

你不須打領帶。

- ✔ It is not necessary for you to wear a tie.

請作出必須的安排。

- ✔ Please make the necessary arrangements.

總之，要減少這類錯誤，我們不應使用中文思維來翻譯為英文，因為中英翻譯不是對號入座那麼簡單的。

4.8 opened 不能用作形容詞

在香港，一些公共洗手間有開放時間的規定，所以這些洗手間的門外通常會寫明開放時間。

例如 Opening hours: 7 a.m. to 9 p.m.

但有人寫成 *The toilet is opened from 7 a.m. to 9 p.m. 那是錯誤的，應改為 The toilet is open from 7 a.m. to 9 p.m. 。為甚麼呢？

原來 open 既是動詞也是形容詞，而 opened 不能作為形容詞使用，它是動詞 open 的過去式和過去分詞 (past participle)，表示「打開」的動作。

例如：

他睜開眼睛起牀。

He opened his eyes and got up.

那大閘被人用鐵筆打開了。

The gate was opened with a cross bar.

銀行明天下午開門嗎？

Are the banks open tomorrow afternoon?

這花園向公眾開放。

The garden is open to the public.

這條路現在可以通行。

The road is open now.

這家超級市場一直營業到晚上十點。

The supermarket is open till 10 p.m.

另外，即使動詞 open 用作「打開」的意思，「打開」的時間只有一個時刻，不可能「由……至……」打開，所以 ✘ The toilet is opened from 7 a.m. to 9 p.m. 不對。

4.9 regret 詞性不同,搭配也不同

相信大家非常熟悉 regret 這個英語詞彙。它是動詞也是名詞,意思跟 sorry 一樣,就是「抱歉、遺憾、後悔」的意思,但 regret 較 sorry 正式及嚴肅一點。尋找工作時最不開心的是面試後收到求職申請失敗的回覆,或合約期滿時收到不獲續約的通知。例如:

我們非常抱歉地通知你,你的申請不成功。

We regret to inform you that your application has not been successful.

我很遺憾地通知你,你的合約不予續簽。

I regret to inform you that your contract will not be renewed.

但以下例子是錯誤的:

她非常遺憾地作出離開的決定。

✘ She bitterly regretted for her decision to leave.

我立刻對我的決定表示遺憾。

✘ I immediately regretted for my decision.

他後悔作出這改變。

✘ He regretted for making this change.

我們對顧客造成的不便表示歉意。

✗ We <u>regret</u> for any inconvenience caused to our customers.

上述例子為甚麼是錯的呢？原來 regret 用作動詞時無需加介詞
for。只有當 regret 用作名詞時才需要加介詞 for。例如：

對於發生的這一切，他深表遺憾。

He has already expressed deep <u>regret</u> for what happened.

她不後悔作出拒絕。

She didn't <u>regret</u> her refusal.

大衛對他的行動不感到遺憾。

David had no <u>regrets</u> for his actions.

他們對未能前來沒有歉意。

They <u>regret</u> being unable to come.

大家也不要把 regret 和 sorry 混淆。例如：

真抱歉給你帶來這麼多麻煩。

I'm <u>sorry</u> for giving you so much trouble.

4.10 sit 和 seat 都可用作動詞

我們學習英語時必須明白各種詞類（parts of speech）的定義及
功能，以便能夠正確運用。

像 <u>sit</u> 是動詞，它的一般意思是「坐」。例如：

坐在這裏。

Sit here.

坐着別動。

Just <u>sit</u> still.

他坐在她旁邊。

He <u>sat</u> beside her.

她坐在書桌前。

She <u>was sitting</u> at her desk.

我坐在岸上。

I <u>sat</u> on the shore.

至於 <u>seat</u>，它一般是名詞，它是「可坐的地方」。例如：

請坐。

Please take a <u>seat</u>.

挨窗戶 / 角落裏的坐位

A window / corner <u>seat</u>

訂位

To book / reserve a <u>seat</u>

注意 <u>seat</u> 有時可用作動詞。例如：

這個體育館能坐一萬人。

The stadium <u>seats</u> 10,000.

他坐在自己的書桌前。

He <u>seated</u> himself at his desk.

Exit Test

總測試

請圈出正確答案。

1 他今年三十歲。

   A He is thirty years of age.

   B He is thirty.

2 她在老年時去世。

   A She died in her old age.

   B She died at an old age.

3 我同意政府的決定。

   A I agreed to the government's decision.

   B I agreed with the government's decision.

4 他們贊成早上十時開會。

   A They agree to meet at 10 a.m.

   B They agree with meet at 10 a.m.

5 總部已安排他們在星期一開始進行工程。

   A The headquarters arranged them to commence the works on Monday.

   B The headquarters arranged for them to commence the works on Monday.

6 我已安排好醫生給她看病。

   A I have arranged for a doctor to see her.

   B I have arranged a doctor to see her.

7 他們的辯解如下。

A Their arguments are as follow.

B Their arguments are as follows.

8 那書的內容如下：

A The content of the book is as follows:

B The content of the book is as follow:

9 吸煙者很清楚吸煙對自己健康的危害。

A Smokers well aware of the hazards to their own health.

B Smokers are well aware of the hazards to their own health.

10 你必須知道你現在所做的是非法的。

A You must aware that what you are doing is illegal.

B You must be aware that what you are doing is illegal.

11 請按以下地址給我寫信。

A Please write to me at the below address.

B Please write to me at the address below.

12 政府應援助那些生活在貧窮線以下的家庭。

A The government should help those families living below the poverty line.

B The government should help those families living the poverty line below.

13 提防陌生人。

A Beware of strangers.

B Take care of strangers.

14 當心遺失金錢。

A Mind your money.

B Beware of losing your money.

15 世界有十億人觀看這場比賽。

A Ten billion people watched the game.

B A billion people watched the game.

16 她認為那肯定值幾十億元。

A She thought that it must be worth billions.

B She thought that it must be worth ten billions.

17 我做了身體檢查。

A I had a body-check.

B I had a physical check-up.

18 她身材健美。

A She has an excellent figure.

B She has an excellent body.

19 已證實該肉適合人食用。

A The meat has been certified fit for human consumption.

B The meat has certified fit for human consumption.

20 他在下午 2 時 14 分被證實死亡。

    A He was certified death at 2:14 pm.

    B He was certified dead at 2:14 pm.

21 我把褲子拿回店裏改一下。

    A I took the trousers back to the shop to have them changed.

    B I took the trousers back to the shop to have them altered.

22 她正要拿這裙子去改。

    A She's having some alterations made to the dress.

    B She's doing some changes to the dress.

23 你必須考慮下一步做甚麼。

    A You have to consider what to do next.

    B You have to consider to do what next.

24 政府應考慮准許他們離開。

    A The government should consider to allow them to leave.

    B The government should consider allowing them to leave.

25 他在工作裏經常與醫生接觸。

    A In his job, he often came into contact with doctors.

    B In his job, he often came into contact doctors.

26 我們一整天都設法與他聯繫。

    A We've been trying to contact with him all day.

    B We've been trying to contact him all day.

27 「恭喜你。」，他說，「你生了個兒子。」

    A "Congratulation", he said, "You have a son."

    B "Congratulations", he said, "You have a son."

28 她寄了一封感謝信給彼德。

    A She sent a letter of thanks to Peter.

    B She sent a letter of thank to Peter.

29 政府受到批評，指其未能控制污染。

    A The government was criticised for failing to control pollution.

    B The government was criticised that they failed to control pollution.

30 專家批評那些建議不夠深入。

    A Experts criticised that the proposals were not going far enough.

    B Experts criticised the proposals for not going far enough.

31 她從舞台的一邊走到另一邊。

    A She walked cross the stage.

    B She walked across the stage.

32 他們乘火車穿過法國。

    A They across France by train.

    B They crossed France by train.

33 他坐在酒吧櫈。

    A He is perching on a bar chair.

    B He is perching on a bar stool.

34 她需要嬰兒櫈。

    A She needs a high chair.

    B She needs a baby chair.

35 讓門關着吧。

    A Keep the door close.

    B Keep the door closed.

36 他們星期日停止營業。

    A They are close on Sundays.

    B They are closed on Sundays.

37 我恐怕陳先生明天上午才會回來。

    A I am afraid Mr. Chan won't come back until tomorrow morning.

    B I am afraid Mr. Chan won't be in until tomorrow morning.

38 她午飯後甚麼時候會返回辦公室工作？

    A When will she come to work after lunch?

    B When will she return to work after lunch?

39 她想有人陪她。

  A She wanted stay with her.

  B She wanted company.

40 我喜歡與你一起。

  A I enjoy your company.

  B I enjoy your together.

41 他們投訴管理層沒有採取行動。

  A They complained the lack of action by the management.

  B They complained about the lack of action by the management.

42 那顧客投訴牛排的質量。

  A The customer complained about the quality of steak.

  B The customer complained the quality of steak.

43 我們對貪污表示極度關注。

  A We very concern about corruption.

  B We are very concerned about corruption.

44 她對房屋問題表示不大關注。

  A She did not show much concern about housing problem.

  B She did not show much concerned about housing problem.

45 她患有嚴重的心臟病。

A She suffers from a serious heart condition.

B She suffers from serious heart conditions.

46 吊車服務將會因惡劣天氣情況而停駛。

A Cable car service will be suspended under adverse weather condition.

B Cable car service will be suspended under adverse weather conditions.

47 我們拿出杯碟來喝茶和咖啡。

A We put out the glasses and saucers for tea and coffee.

B We put out the cups and saucers for tea and coffee.

48 她把酒杯拿走。

A She took away the wine glass.

B She took away the wine cup.

49 她的名譽受到很大的傷害。

A The damages to her reputation is considerable.

B The damage to her reputation is considerable.

50 過度日曬會對皮膚造成嚴重損傷。

A Too much sun can do damage to your skin.

B Too much sun can do damages to your skin.

51 我與牙醫有約。

A I have a date with the dentist.

B I have an appointment with the dentist.

52 他約了她出去。

A He asked her out on a date.

B He asked her out on the date.

53 她要求立即解釋。

A She demanded an immediate explanation.

B She demanded for an immediate explanation.

54 你可以要求一份免費單張。

A You can request for a free copy of the leaflet.

B You can request a free copy of the leaflet.

55 電池完全沒電，所以車子發動不了。

A The car won't start because the battery will be completely dead.

B The car won't start because the battery was completely dead.

56 我想她已經死了。

A I'm afraid she is dead.

B I'm afraid she was dead.

57 議員對明年的計劃進行了詳細討論。

A Members had a detailed discussion about the plans for next year.

B Members had a detailed discussion the plans for next year.

58 他們拒絕跟他討論這個問題。

A They refused to discuss about it with him.

B They refused to discuss it with him.

59 你知道他住在哪裏？

A Do you know where does he live?

B Do you know where he lives?

60 我不知道她甚麼時候到達。

A I don't know when she will arrive.

B I don't know when will she arrive.

61 由於機場罷工，貨物供應延誤了。

A Supplies have been delayed due to a strike at the airport.

B Supplies have been delayed because a strike at the airport.

62 公司繼續發工資給那些因病缺勤的職員。

A The company continues to pay the wages of the staff who are absent was due to illness.

B The company continues to pay the wages of the staff who are absent due to illness.

63 他已經辭職，由一月一日起生效。

A He has resigned with effect from 1 January.

B He has resigned with effective from 1 January.

64 規則由半夜起生效。

A The rules become effect at midnight.

B The rules become effective at midnight.

65 你父母移居國外多久？

A How long ago did your parents immigrate?

B How long ago did your parents emigrate?

66 通過入境處櫃台之後，你便可以去取行李了。

A After you have gone through the emigration counter, you can go and get your luggage.

B After you have gone through the immigration counter, you can go and get your luggage.

67 我們與該部門簽訂了協議。

A We have entered an agreement with the department.

B We have entered into an agreement with the department.

68 該製造商計劃進入香港市場。

A The manufacturer plans to enter the Hong Kong market.

B The manufacturer plans to entry the Hong Kong market.

69 她需要一本常用小詞典。

A She needs a small dictionary for every day use.

B She needs a small dictionary for everyday use.

70 免費泊車優惠有效時間由每天上午 8 時至晚上 11 時。

A Free parking privilege is valid from 8 a.m. to 11 p.m. everyday.

B Free parking privilege is valid from 8 a.m. to 11 p.m. every day.

71 除了約翰和瑪莉以外，誰也沒有來。

A Except for John and Mary, nobody came.

B Except John and Mary, nobody came.

72 除了他以外，人人都懂。

A Everybody understood except him.

B Everybody understood except he.

73 我的護照將在明年到期。

A My passport will expire next year.

B My passport will be expired next year.

74 他的遊客簽證昨天期滿。

A His visitor's visa was expired yesterday.

B His visitor's visa expired yesterday.

75 不要忘記交電費。

A Do not forget to pay the electricity fee.

B Do not forget to pay the electricity bill.

76 駕駛執照的費用快將增加。

A The fee for a driving licence is going up soon.

B The expense for a driving licence is going up soon.

77 培訓的預約有限，先到先得。

A Reservations for training are subject to availability on a first-come-first-served basis.

B Reservations for training are subject to availability on a first-come-first-serve basis.

78 我們將會以先到先得方式與你聯絡。

A We will contact you on a first come, first serve basis.

B We will contact you on a first come, first served basis.

79 他把筆掉在課室的地上。

A He dropped the pen on the ground in the classroom.

B He dropped the pen on the floor in the classroom.

80 下雨後，足球場的地面通常是濕的。

A The ground of the soccer pitch was usually wet after the rain.

B The floor of the soccer pitch was usually wet after the rain.

81 結果如下：

    A   The results are followings:

    B   The results are follows:

82 以下哪一項是真實的？

    A   Which of the following is true?

    B   Which of the followings is true?

83 不要忘記付款。

    A   Don't forget paying.

    B   Don't forget to pay.

84 我忘記在舞會見過她。

    A   I forget seeing her in the dancing party.

    B   I forget to see her in the dancing party.

85 將來很有希望。

    A   There is high hope in future.

    B   There is high hope in the future.

86 以後避免這一點。

    A   Avoid it in future.

    B   Avoid it in the future.

87 The price of houses ... risen sharply.

    A   have

    B   has

88 I think that economics ... difficult.

A are

B is

89 None of their replies ... correct.

A is

B are

90 該項目在 2000 年完成。

A The project has been completed in 2000.

B The project was completed in 2000.

91 我們收到你 7 月 15 日的來信。

A We have received your letter of 15 July.

B We received your letter of 15 July.

92 你必須做完所有家課。

A You must finish all your homework.

B You must finish all your homeworks.

93 警察總部當時有一百人。

A There were one hundred peoples in the police headquarter.

B There were one hundred people in the police headquarters.

94 請幫忙抬一下這沉重的行李好嗎？

A Could you give me a hand with this heavy luggage, please?

B Could you give me hands with this heavy luggage, please?

95 她從丈夫聽到這事。

A She heard about it at first hand from her husband.

B She heard about it at first hands from her husband.

96 你可以即時上班嗎？

A Are you immediate available?

B Are you immediately available?

97 情況很明顯，這裏存在某種問題。

A It was immediately obvious that there was some kind of problem.

B It was immediate obvious that there was some kind of problem.

98 你知道現在要買一個小住宅單位要多少錢嗎？

Do you know how much... to buy a small flat now?

A does it cost

B it costs

99 他想知道今天我們會做甚麼？

He wants to know what... today.

A will we do

B we will do

100 我當時知道他們怎樣回應。

I knew how...

A they responded

B did they respond

101 科學家正在探究癌症的病因。

A Scientists are investigating into the causes of cancer.

B Scientists are investigating the causes of cancer.

102 警方正在調查這宗罪行。

A The police are conducting investigation into the crime.

B The police are conducting investigation the crime.

103 請把鹽遞來。

A Please kindly pass the salt.

B Please pass the salt.

104 請把它放回原處。

A Please put it back.

B Please kindly put it back.

105 他缺乏勇氣去幹。

A He lacks of courage to do it.

B He lacks courage to do it.

106 你缺乏的是堅毅。

A What you lack is perseverance.

B What you lack of is perseverance.

107 你最近甚麼時候見到過她？

A When did you last see her?

B When did you see her the last?

108 最後一組人構成嚴重的威脅。

A The last group poses a serious threat.

B Last group poses a serious threat.

109 她不是躺在牀上。

A She is not lying on the bed.

B She does not lying on the bed.

110 請不要在入口等候。

A Please do not waiting at the entrance.

B Please do not wait at the entrance.

111 門已鎖上。

A The door has locked.

B The door has been locked.

112 這門鎖不上。

A This door won't lock.

B This door won't be locked.

113 去年銷量增加 5%。

A　Sales were increased by 5 per cent last year.

B　Sales increased by 5 per cent last year.

114 上季汽車罪案顯著下降。

A　Car crime was fallen significantly last quarter.

B　Car crime fell significantly last quarter.

115 盼覆。

A　I look forward to hear from you.

B　I look forward to hearing from you.

116 我們非常盼望能再見到你。

A　We are really looking forward to seeing you again.

B　We are really looking forward to see you again.

117 她低頭才能過這道門。

A　She lowered down her head to get through the door.

B　She lowered her head to get through the door.

118 銀行把利率降低了 3 厘。

A　The bank has lowered interest rates by 3 percent.

B　The bank has low down interest rates by 3 percent.

119 討論已記錄在會議記錄中。

A The discussion was recorded in the minutes of the meeting.

B The discussion was recorded in the minute of the meeting.

120 有些議題已在其他議程中討論。

A Some of the issues were discussed under other agendas.

B Some of the issues were discussed under other agenda items.

121 你不一定要出席這會議。

A You may not need to attend the meeting.

B You are necessary to attend the meeting.

122 她可能需要做手術。

A She may be necessary to have an operation.

B It may be necessary for her to have an operation.

123 第二天他們獲得釋放。

A Next day they were released.

B The next day they were released.

124 希望下星期再見。

A Hope to see you next week.

B Hope to see you the next week.

125 他從不抽煙、也不喝酒。

　　A　He never smokes and drinks.

　　B　He never smokes or drinks.

126 她一整天既沒吃、也沒喝。

　　A　She's had nothing to eat and drink all day.

　　B　She's had nothing to eat or drink all day.

127 請注意，所有旅客必須持有效護照。

　　A　Please be noted that all travellers must have a valid passport.

　　B　Please note that all travellers must have a valid passport.

128 請留意：泊車位有限。

　　A　Please note that there are a limited number of parking spaces.

　　B　Please be noted that there are a limited number of parking spaces.

129 只有 2 % 的病人出現併發症。

　　A　Complications are occurred in only 2 % of patients.

　　B　Complications occurred in only 2 % of patients.

130 接下來的一小時內甚麼事都可能會發生。

　　A　Anything could happen in the next hour.

　　B　Anything could be happened in the next hour.

131 大火在上星期日晚上發生。

A The fire occurred in the night of last Sunday.

B The fire occurred on the night of last Sunday.

132 警方將在下星期一採取行動。

A The police will take action next Monday.

B The police will take action on next Monday.

133 那商店星期一至星期六都營業。

A The shop is opened Monday through Saturday.

B The shop is open Monday through Saturday.

134 這洗手間不對外開放。

A The toilet is not open to the public.

B The toilet is not opened to the public.

135 請列出你們最喜愛的歌曲。

A Please list out your favourite songs.

B Please list your favourite songs.

136 他們表示支持國際援助。

A They voiced support for international assistance.

B They voiced out support for international assistance.

137 那沙井蓋在哪裏？

A Where is the sand well cover?

B Where is the manhole cover?

138 那些水馬還沒移走。

A The water-billed barriers have not been removed.

B The water barriers have not been removed.

139 我想加上另一原因。

A I would like to add up another reason.

B I would like to add another reason.

140 請列出顧客的姓名。

A Please list the names of the customers.

B Please list out the names of the customers.

141 需要不同措施改善毒品問題。

A Different measures are needed to reduce the drug problem.

B Different measures are needed to improve the drug problem.

142 她需要改善嚴重健康問題。

A She has to improve her serious health problem.

B She has to reduce her serious health problem.

143 醉駕是導致交通意外的原因之一。

A Drink driving is one of the reasons of traffic accidents.

B Drink driving is one of the causes of traffic accidents.

144 我為甚麼要幫他？給我一個充份的理由。

A Give me a good reason why I should help him.

B Give me a good cause why I should help him.

145 我們對延誤帶來的不便感到遺憾。

A We regretted for any inconvenience caused by the delay.

B We regretted any inconvenience caused by the delay.

146 他不後悔移居香港。

A He doesn't regret moving to Hong Kong.

B He doesn't regret for moving to Hong Kong.

147 記得寄信。

A Please remember to post the letter.

B Please remember posting the letter.

148 我想起在會議見過他們。

A I remember seeing them at the meeting.

B I remember to see them at the meeting.

149 據報他失蹤了。

A He reported missing.

B He was reported missing.

150 該謀殺案在所有報章都有報導。

A The murder was reported in all the newspapers.

B The murder reported in all the newspapers.

151 我還沒有回覆約翰的信。

   A I've not replied John's letter yet.

   B I've not replied to John's letter yet.

152 她會早日回覆他們。

   A She will reply as soon as possible.

   B She will reply them as soon as possible.

153 我願再做同樣的事。

   A I would do same again.

   B I would do the same again.

154 男孩、女孩，我們的對待一樣。

   A We treat boys exactly same as girls.

   B We treat boys exactly the same as girls.

155 我在後座。

   A I was in the back sit.

   B I was in the back seat.

156 他坐在椅子上。

   A He was sitting on a chair.

   B He was seating on a chair.

157 Dear Sir / Madam, ... 結束語是

   A Yours faithfully,

   B Yours sincerely,

158 Dear Ms Chan, ... 結束語是

A Yours faithfully,

B Yours sincerely,

159 價錢從 2 元起。

A Prices start from $2.

B Prices start at $2.

160 我覺得我們應該六點鐘出發。

A I think we ought to start at six.

B I think we ought to start from six.

161 你的申請不成功。

A Your application is not successful.

B Your application is not succeeded.

162 很少有人能成功減肥。

A Very few people succeed to lose weight.

B Very few people succeed in losing weight.

163 她建議他去看醫生。

A She suggested that he should see a doctor.

B She suggested that him to see a doctor.

164 我提議你先打電話給她。

A I suggest you to call her first.

B I suggest you call her first.

165 停車場暫時關閉。

A The carpark is temporary closed.

B The carpark is temporarily closed.

166 升降機暫停服務。

A Lift service is temporarily suspended.

B Lift service is temporary suspended.

167 她很迷亂。

A She is confusing.

B She is confused.

168 那交通擠塞令人惱火。

A The traffic congestion was annoying.

B The traffic congestion was annoyed.

169 感謝你的批准。

A Thank your approval.

B Thank you for your approval.

170 感謝你的諒解。

A Thank you for your understanding.

B Thanks your understanding.

171 工人需要技能培訓更新。

A The workers need updating of skills training.

B The workers need upgrading of skills training.

172 名單將會更新。

A The list will be updated periodically.

B The list will be renewed periodically.

173 他等候面試，所以很緊張。

A He was very tense as he waited for the interview.

B He was very tense as he waited the interview.

174 請在圖書館外面等我。

A Please wait me outside the library.

B Please wait for me outside the library.

175 他們想試就試試吧。

A They're most welcomed to try.

B They're most welcome to try.

176 她歡迎新員工。

A She is welcomed the new staff.

B She welcomed the new staff.

177 這做法很受歡迎。

A This approach was well received.

B This approach well received.

178 收到電郵，感謝。

A Receive with thanks.

B Received with thanks.

179 He's got nice...

   A glass

   B glasses

180 What's the latest... ?

   A news

   B new

181 We need to buy some brand new computer...

   A equipments

   B equipment

182 I want more...

   A papers

   B paper

183 天氣對我們的計劃有利。

   A The weather is favourable to our scheme.

   B The weather is in favour of our scheme.

184 他們投票贊成該決議。

   A They voted in favour of the resolution.

   B They voted favourable to the resolution.

185 最惠國

   A The most favourite nation

   B The most favoured nation

186 豆腐是他最喜愛吃的東西。

A Tofu is his favourite.

B Tofu is his most favourite.

187 它實用而且優雅，顯然是設計的典範。

A Practical and gracious, it is a clear example of design.

B Practical and graceful, it is a clear example of design.

188 她勤奮又可親。

A She is a hardworking and gracious person.

B She is a hardworking and graceful person.

189 由於仍在保用期內，他們將會修理這電腦。

A They would repair the computer as it was still under guarantee.

B They would repair the computer as it was still in guarantee.

190 如需在保用之中進行修理，請確保出示收據。

A In the event of a repair in guarantee, please make sure to present a receipt.

B In the event of a repair under guarantee, please make sure to present a receipt.

191 我們聘請一家顧問公司來設計新系統。

A We rented a firm of consultants to design our new system.

B We hired a firm of consultants to design our new system.

192 他在沙田租了一個單位。

A He rented a flat in Shatin.

B He hired a flat in Shatin.

193 這界限是虛構的。

A The boundary is imaginative.

B The boundary is imaginary.

194 我們需要充滿想像力的構想。

A We need imaginative conception.

B We need imaginary conception.

195 她是不會說謊的。

A She is incapable to lie.

B She is incapable of lying.

196 他沒有從他的過錯得到教訓。

A He is incapable of learning from his mistakes.

B He is incapable to learn from his mistakes.

197 客人可選擇在戶外坐或在私人房間裏享用美食。

A Diners have a choice of outdoor seating or private room.

B Diners have a choice of outdoors seating or private room.

198 他們正在室內暖水池游泳。

A They are swimming in the indoors heated pool.

B They are swimming in the indoor heated pool.

199 這些產品比我們去年買的差。

A These products are inferior than those we bought last year.

B These products are inferior to those we bought last year.

200 他們是否比其他選項便宜和質量差？

A Are they cheap and inferior to other options?

B Are they cheap and inferior than other options?

201 會議將由六個月一次改為三個月一次。

A The meeting will be held every three instead to six months.

B The meeting will be held every three instead of six months.

202 聘用了顧問，而不是臨時職員。

A Consultants were used instead of temporary staff.

B Consultants were used instead to temporary staff.

203 我不想打擾你們家。

A I don't want to intrude your family.

B I don't want to intrude on your family.

204 有些女士會覺得受到了侵擾。

A Some women would feel intruded.

B Some women would feel intruded upon.

205 她不會講笑話。

A She can't say jokes.

B She can't tell jokes.

206 他們經常互相取笑。

A They often make jokes at each other's expense.

B They often say jokes at each other's expense.

207 行李廂

A Luggages compartment

B Luggage compartment

208 把一些行李和其他物品存入倉庫裏。

A Some luggage and other items were stored at the warehouse.

B Some luggages and other items were stored at the warehouse.

209 He let his wife _____ all his financial affairs.

A manage

B arrange

210 It took just a few days to _____ travel documents.

A arrange for

B manage

211 我認為在這裏我們會遇到難題。

A I think we have a problem here.

B I think we have a matter here.

212 你的手怎麼啦？

A What is the problem with your hand?

B What is the matter with your hand?

213 她記住了她所有朋友的電話號碼。

A She has remembered all her friends' telephone number.

B She has memorised all her friends' telephone number.

214 我記不起我把汽車停在哪裏了。

A I can't remember where I parked my car.

B I can't memorise where I parked my car.

215 我剛開始除草小狗就走過來。

A No sooner I had started mowing than the puppy came over.

B No sooner had I started mowing than the puppy came over.

216 問題在一區剛消失就在另一區出現。

A No sooner had the problem died down in one district than it cropped up in another.

B No sooner the problem died down in one district than it cropped up in another.

217 他不得不解釋清楚。

A　He felt obliged to explain clearly.

B　It obliged him to explain clearly.

218 他們必須準時繳交會費。

A　It obliged them to pay membership fees on time.

B　They are obliged to pay membership fees on time.

219 火車已晚點 20 分鐘。

A　The train is 20 minutes overdue.

B　The train is 20 minutes expired.

220 他的任期 12 月底屆滿。

A　His term of office expires at the end of December.

B　His term of office is overdue at the end of December.

221 每個人的基因密碼都是獨有的。

A　Each person's genetic code is unique.

B　Each person's genetic code is very unique.

222 他的繪畫風格非常獨特。

A　His painting style is so unique.

B　His painting style is unique.

223 從她公寓的窗向外看去可見到倫敦的絕妙景色。

A　The windows of her flat looked out on to a superb view of London.

B The windows of her flat looked out on to a superb sight of London.

224 年度花卉展覽上的鮮花賞心悦目。

A The flowers at the annual flower show were a beautiful view.

B The flowers at the annual flower show were a beautiful sight.

225 他為甚麼這麼輕聲説話？

A Why did he speak with such a low voice?

B Why did he speak in such a low voice?

226 有時，聲音較小的聽從了聲音較大的人。

A Sometimes, those speaking in a low voice would obey those in a loud voice.

B Sometimes, those speaking with a low voice would obey those with a loud voice.

Answers

答案

1 B	25 A	49 B	73 A
2 A	26 B	50 A	74 B
3 B	27 B	51 B	75 B
4 A	28 A	52 A	76 A
5 B	29 A	53 A	77 A
6 A	30 B	54 B	78 B
7 B	31 B	55 B	79 B
8 A	32 B	56 A	80 B
9 B	33 B	57 A	81 B
10 B	34 A	58 B	82 A
11 B	35 B	59 B	83 B
12 A	36 B	60 A	84 A
13 A	37 B	61 A	85 B
14 B	38 B	62 B	86 A
15 B	39 B	63 A	87 B
16 A	40 A	64 B	88 B
17 B	41 B	65 B	89 B
18 A	42 A	66 B	90 B
19 A	43 B	67 B	91 A
20 B	44 A	68 A	92 A
21 B	45 A	69 B	93 B
22 A	46 B	70 B	94 A
23 A	47 B	71 A	95 A
24 B	48 A	72 A	96 B

97 A	121 A	145 B	169 B
98 B	122 B	146 A	170 A
99 B	123 B	147 A	171 B
100 A	124 A	148 A	172 A
101 B	125 B	149 B	173 A
102 A	126 B	150 A	174 B
103 B	127 B	151 B	175 B
104 A	128 A	152 A	176 B
105 B	129 B	153 B	177 A
106 A	130 A	154 B	178 B
107 A	131 B	155 B	179 B
108 A	132 A	156 A	180 A
109 A	133 B	157 A	181 B
110 B	134 A	158 B	182 B
111 B	135 B	159 B	183 A
112 B	136 A	160 A	184 A
113 B	137 B	161 A	185 B
114 B	138 A	162 B	186 A
115 B	139 B	163 A	187 B
116 A	140 A	164 B	188 A
117 B	141 A	165 B	189 A
118 A	142 B	166 A	190 B
119 A	143 B	167 B	191 B
120 B	144 A	168 A	192 A

193 B	203 B	213 B	223 A
194 A	204 B	214 A	224 B
195 B	205 B	215 B	225 B
196 A	206 A	216 A	226 A
197 A	207 B	217 A	
198 B	208 A	218 B	
199 B	209 A	219 A	
200 A	210 A	220 A	
201 B	211 A	221 A	
202 A	212 B	222 B	

主要參考書目

Alexandra, Louis. *Longman English Grammar*. New York: Longman Inc., 1988.

Boyle, Joseph and Linda. *Common Spoken English Errors in Hong Kong*. Hong Kong: Longman Group (Far East) Limited, 1991.

Bunton, David. *Common English Errors in Hong Kong*. Hong Kong: Longman Group (Far East) Limited, 1989.

Bunton, David. *More Common English Errors in Hong Kong*. Hong Kong: Pearson, 2011.

Bunton, David. *Common Social English Errors in Hong Kong*. Hong Kong: Longman, 1996.

Jenkins, George. *English Problem Words*. Hong Kong: The Commercial Press, 1994.

Potter, John. *Common Business English Errors in Hong Kong*, Hong Kong: Addison Wesley Longman China Limited, 1992

Quirk, Randolph, et al. *A Comprehensive Grammar of the English Language*. London: Longman Group Limited, 1985.

Reader's Digest Association Limited. *The Right Word at the Right Time*. London: Reader's Digest Association Limited, 1985.

Sinclair, John. *Collins COBUILD English Usage*. London: Williams Collins Sons & Co. Ltd., 1992.

Sinclair, John. *Collins COBUILD English Language Dictionary*.

London: Williams Collins Sons & Co. Ltd., 2000.

Swan, Michael. *Practical English Usage*. London: Oxford University Press, 2010.

Thomson, A. J. and Martinet A. V. *A Practical English Grammar* (Fourth Edition). London: Oxford University Press, 1986.

Turton, Nigel, D. *Correct Usage in Written English*. Hong Kong: The Commercial Press, 1990.

方廷鈺、鷹志譯。《英語常用語法詞典》。北京：外語教學與研究出版社，1984。

外語教學與研究出版社、英國培生教育出版亞洲有限公司。《朗文當代高級英語辭典：英英・英漢雙解》。北京：外語教學與研究出版社，2014。

外語教學與研究出版社、劍橋大學出版社。《劍橋高階英漢雙解詞典》。北京：外語教學與研究出版社，2008。

外語教學與研究出版社、麥克米倫出版社。《麥克米倫高級英漢雙解詞典》。香港：商務印書館 (香港) 有限公司、麥克米倫出版社，2008。

牛津大學出版社。《牛津高階英漢雙解詞典》。北京：商務印書館、牛津大學出版社，2013。

沙昭宇、周敬華。《英語正誤句解》。河北：人民出版社，1981。

吳拓、楊應鵬譯。《英美語慣用法辭典》。湖南：湖南師範大學出版社，1991。

周少明、王卿譯。《實用英語正誤手冊》。上海：知識出版社，

1987。

約翰辛克萊主編、任紹曾主譯。《英語語法大全》。香港：商務印書館（香港）有限公司，1998。

施玉惠編。《英文作文翻譯典型錯誤》。台北：四庫圖書公司。

黃雪蓉編。No More Chinglish，香港：香港經濟日報，2008。

朗文詞典編譯出版部。《朗文當代高級辭典》。香港：朗文出版亞洲有限公司，1997。

朗文辭書／翻譯出版部。《朗文常用英語正誤詞典》。香港：朗文出版 (遠東) 有限公司，1990。

張道真編。《現代英語用法詞典 (重排本)》。北京：外語教學與研究出版社，1994。

張道真編。《實用英語語法》。北京：商務印書館，1995。

張瑞璧、夏建明譯。《英語中常見的錯誤》。福建：人民出版社，1983。

陸谷孫主編。《英漢大詞典》。上海：上海譯文出版社，1989。

陸谷孫主編。《COBUILD 英漢雙解詞典》。上海：上海譯文出版社，2002。

孫述宇、金聖華。《英譯中：英漢翻譯概論》。香港：香港中文大學校外進修部，1975。

陳定安。《英漢比較與翻譯》。香港：商務印書館，1985。

葉青。《基本英語句子結構》。香港：商務印書館，1975。

楊霞華主編。《英語正誤辨析詞典》。上海：上海外語教育出版社，

1999。

葛傳槼。《葛傳槼英語慣用法詞典》。上海：上海譯文出版社，2012。

葛傳槼。《簡明英語慣用法》。上海：上海譯文出版社，1993。

薄冰。《薄冰英語語法》。北京：開明出版社，1999。

錢歌川。《英文疑難詳解》。北京：中國對外翻譯出版公司，1981。

錢歌川。《英文疑難詳解續篇》。北京：中國對外翻譯出版公司，1981。

劉毅主編。《英文正誤用法辭典》。台北：學習出版公司，1987。

嚴維明。《英語語法速遞》。香港：商務印書館，1998。